Journey North

By Carol Hall

Front cover photo by Carol Hall

This book is dedicated to God, first and foremost. He gave me this story in a dream.

I also want to thank my beloved husband, Kerry Hall and my twin sister, Carla Plew for always encouraging me and supporting me in my writing endeavors. I love you both more than words can say.

CHAPTER 1

Summer 1864

The carriage jostled and bounced over the rutted dirt road. It was hot even for July and the smell of the sweaty horses hung heavy in the air. Dust drifted up from the road and swirled around them as they sped down the road.

Thirteen year old Emily Dunn sat on the seat across from Mr. Cordell without saying a word. They had been traveling for several days now and Emily was tired and bored.

She peered out the window and watched the trees fly by as she thought of her father and wondered if he was ok.

Her father, Glen Monroe Dunn, owned and operated a large iron manufacturing company in Pennsylvania called Dunn Iron Works. Since he traveled a lot on business, Emily was left in the care of her nanny, Olive Douley, most of the time.

Olive rarely knew where Emily was. She was always fussing about the house looking after the laundry or cleaning up some imagined mess. She didn't have time for Emily, aside from her daily school work. Emily had the run of the expansive house and property and spent most of her time outdoors.

On the day Mr. Cordell had come to get her, Emily had been playing near the small stream that ran through the backyard of the property. When he had approached her, he told her that her father had been in an accident while away on business and he was sent to fetch her and take her to him.

Stunned by the news, Emily insisted that she run inside and tell Olive what had happened and that she was leaving, but Mr. Cordell assured her there was no time, they must leave immediately.

Scared and unsure of what to do, Emily had taken his proffered hand and let him lead her to a carriage that was waiting just down the road and around a corner from her home.

The carriage was plain with black painted sides and red trim. Curtains of red and gold hung over the windows. Two sturdy looking horses were hitched up to the front of the carriage, stamping their feet and chewing on their bits.

As Mr. Cordell opened the door for her, she took note of a small square luggage case that sat on one of the seats. She realized she hadn't had time to pack herself a trunk and turned to tell Mr. Cordell, but he quickly ushered her inside.

She scrambled up onto one of the leather seats.

As soon as Mr. Cordell shut the door, he knocked on the roof of the carriage to signal the driver it was time to go.

The carriage jerked into motion and they headed down the street away from the town.

That was ten days ago and Emily wondered how much farther they had to go. Surely her father wouldn't have traveled this far for business? She just hoped he would be ok until she got to him, wherever he was.

The carriage rocked back and forth and soon, it lulled Emily to sleep.

Sometime later, the carriage jolted hard to one side, jarring Emily from her sleep. She sat up in her seat and looked over at Mr. Cordell. He was leaning back on the seat looking at his pocket watch.

"Mr. Cordell," Emily said. "Are we almost there yet?"

"Actually, Miss Emily, we are," he said, clicking the watch closed and stuffing it back into his vest pocket.

"Where exactly are we?"

"We're in southern Virginia."

"Southern Virginia?" Emily asked, aghast. "Why would my father be in southern Virginia? He works with northern companies only."

"Don't you worry about it, Miss Emily," Mr. Cordell said in that infuriating tone he used when he didn't want to answer her questions. "Just sit back and relax. We'll be arriving at our destination within the hour."

Emily was relieved to hear this. She didn't relish the idea of spending another night in a roadside inn again. Mr. Cordell always took the bed, leaving Emily to sleep on the floor. Their meager breakfasts usually consisted of dried toast and warm milk. Something she was not accustomed to. Olive always made the best breakfasts of warm flapjacks, fresh fruit and hot tea. Emily's stomach growled just thinking about it.

True to his word, about an hour later, the carriage began to slow it's pace. Emily pulled the curtain aside to see where they were and was shocked to see nothing but fields and pastures all around them.

She turned abruptly to Mr. Cordell with a questioning look on her face. He simply nodded at her and patted her knee.

"Mr. Cordell," she asked. "Where are we? Where's the town? Where's my father?"

"Don't you worry about anything," he said, tapping on the roof of the carriage to signal the driver to stop. "You'll be just fine."

"What do you mean I'll be just fine?" she asked, feeling a prickle of fear in her stomach. "Why wouldn't I be?"

"You'll learn what you need to know soon enough. Now enough chitter chatter. Brush your hair down a bit and straighten out your dress. I want you to look presentable."

Emily smoothed the front of her floral printed dress down with her hands, letting his words sink in. She was totally confused by what he said, but didn't know what to say to him.

The carriage came to a stop. Emily pulled the curtain aside and gazed out into a large open pasture. A dilapidated barn sat a ways off, looking lonely and forlorn. No animals were present and she didn't see a house anywhere in sight.

Mr. Cordell swung the door open and stepped down onto the road. He made a loud whistling noise, then turned back to the carriage.

"Come on down now, Miss Emily," he said.

The step down was a big one and without his help, she would have surely fallen on her face. He lifted her by her waist and set her down next to him.

Once she was on the ground, he began fluffing her curly, waist length, blond hair. He was squeezing the curls and twisting them around his fingers to bring out as much of the curl as possible. He then began to smooth her dress down and adjust her skirt and collar.

Emily stood there dumbly, wondering what in the world he was doing and why. She slapped at his hand though, when he began to reach down toward her stockings.

"Excuse me, sir!" she said, aghast at his boldness. "What do you think you are doing?"

"I told you to make yourself presentable. I am merely helping you do that."

"I want to go to my father now. Surely he is not here. Why have we stopped here anyway?"

"Hush now, child," he said, giving her hair one more fluffing.

Emily took in her surroundings and noticed a man approaching them from the direction of the old barn.

"Someone's coming," she said.

"Ah, good. Took him long enough."

"Who is he?"

"Don't worry about that right now. You'll find out soon enough. Now, stand up straight and mind your manners when he gets here."

Emily watched the man make his way toward them. When he was close enough, she could see he was rather slovenly and somewhat overweight. She didn't have a good feeling about this. Where was her father? Who was this man approaching them? Why had they stopped here?

When the man finally got to them, he held out his meaty, dirty hand for Mr. Cordell to shake.

"Everything go ok, James?" he asked, addressing Mr. Cordell. "No problems?"

"None at all, sir. It was an uneventful trip, albeit, long."

"Well, we can't be getting them from around here, now can we?" the man asked, chuckling.

"No, I suppose not," said Mr. Cordell.

The man was looking Emily up and down like she was a prized bull. Emily blushed and tried to step behind Mr. Cordell, who promptly placed his hand on her back and shoved her forward toward the man.

"Well? What do you think?" he asked the man. "She's a real beauty isn't she? She'll bring you a fair price."

Emily balked at that remark. She swung around to face Mr. Cordell. Fear etched into her face.

"What do you mean I'll bring him a fair price? Where's my father. I insist you take me to him at once!

"Your father?" the man asked, then looked at Mr. Cordell. "What's this about?"

"That's the story I told her the day I picked her up," Mr. Cordell said. "I told her that her father was injured at work and I was sent to get her and take her to him. She easily believed me and came along quietly."

Emily's mouth dropped open at this new revelation. What? Her father really wasn't hurt? He wasn't even here?

Emily took a step backward as if to turn and run, but Mr. Cordell quickly grabbed her arm and squeezed.

"Oh no you don't. You're going to go with this fellow. His name is Johnathan Guthrie. Now you be a good girl and don't go giving him any trouble, you hear," he said, shaking her slightly.

"No," Emily said. "I will not go with him. Take me home at once!"

Both men laughed.

Mr. Cordell handed her over to Mr. Guthrie who took her firmly by the arm and gave her a rough shake.

"Now listen here, missy," he told her, growling in her ear. "There'll be no haughtiness out of you, you understand? You do what I tell you and we'll get along just fine. You don't and you'll be sorry, got it?"

His face was close to hers and she could smell a foul odor on his breath. She cringed back from him and nodded.

"Here's your payment, James," Mr. Guthrie said, handing Mr. Cordell a wad of bills. "You keep bringing me little gems like this one and you could end up a rich man."

Mr. Cordell tipped his hat at Mr. Guthrie and smiled. "Yes sir. It was my pleasure."

He turned and hoisted himself back up into the carriage. With a nod at Emily, he tapped the roof and the carriage took off down the dirt road.

Mr. Guthrie jerked Emily's arm and pulled her along with him as he walked back toward the barn.

"Where are we going, sir?" Emily asked. She didn't try to pull away from him. She was too terrified to do anything but follow along.

"You, my dear, belong to my little band of girls now. You're on your way south to become a slave to a rich plantation owner. You're gonna fetch me a mighty fine price too, being so pretty and all."

"What do you mean a slave? I'm not a colored girl!"

"You northerners are robbing us of our slaves, so we're collecting a bunch of you to take the place of the ones we've lost. Now come along. I got work to do."

He dragged her across the pasture toward the barn. Though she tripped and stumbled several times trying to keep up, he never slowed his pace. The grip he had on her arm was beginning to hurt, but she didn't offer up any complaint. She just let him drag her along until they reached the barn.

Fear crawled up her spine and a wave of nausea washed over her. She was in big trouble and didn't know what to do about it. Where was her father? She knew now he wasn't hurt and hadn't sent for her. He must be worried sick. What would he do when he realized she was gone? How would she get back home? What was going to happen to her?

Her mind whirled with all these thoughts, but none was more pressing than the thought of what horrible fate awaited her.

CHAPTER 2

The barn was ram-shackled and falling apart. The smell of moldy hay and rotting wood filled Emily's nostrils as they entered the barn.

In the dim light of the interior, Emily could make out four stalls and a hayloft overhead. There were several men sitting around on old barrels playing cards and drinking what Emily assumed was probably whiskey. Her father had told her tales of men who liked to gamble on their cards and drink strong drinks while doing it. She had a much clearer picture of what he was talking about now.

She averted her eyes away from the men and focused on Mr. Guthrie. He paused in front of one of the stalls and peered inside, then seemed to change his mind and moved on to the next one. He gazed inside, then quickly jerked her around til she was in front of it.

"You'll be in this one," he said, as he shoved her inside.

She staggered into the small enclosure and turned quickly back to look at Mr. Guthrie.

"What are you going to do with me?" she asked.

"Nothing for now," he responded, sticking a piece of straw between his teeth. "You'll stay in here til morning when we head out."

"Where exactly are we going, sir?"

"I told you already. South."

With that, he grabbed the stall door by the handle and slid it closed. Emily heard a lock slide into place and click closed.

She inspected her small prison. Though it was rather dark and shadowy, she could see it had four solid walls. The roof, however, had several holes in it that she could see daylight through. Old straw covered the floor and cobwebs hung from every corner. It smelled dank and musty. The door was solid on the bottom and had bars at the top. Through the bars, she could see the men still sitting out in the aisle playing cards.

She turned and made her way to the corner closest to her and sat down. She drew her knees up to her chest and wrapped her arms around her legs.

The afternoon wore on and with it clouds began to form. Emily could see the light fading outside through the holes in the ceiling. It looked like a storm was coming.

She closed her eyes and laid her head on her knees and began to cry. She was so scared and missed her father. Oh what she would give to be at home right now. She imagined the fine feast Olive would have prepared for dinner. The hot bath she would have enjoyed, then snuggling down into her large feather bed with all her handmade quilts. A large tear escaped her eye and slowly slid down her cheek.

Darkness fell, bringing with it heavy rain, thunder and lightning. Emily squeezed herself into the corner as far as she could get, but there was no escaping the rain that dripped down on her from the holes in the roof.

She glanced up at the ceiling and let out a long, deep sigh. She pulled her dress farther down over her legs to help keep the chill off of her. It may be springtime, but storms always made the air chilly, even, apparently, in Virginia.

As she lowered her head back down and gazed around the room, she suddenly stopped and gasped. Across the room in the corner diagonal from where she sat, she saw a pair of white orbs staring in her direction. She blinked several times, but the orbs continued to stare at her.

"Hello?" she whispered softly. "Are you a ghost?"

A responding giggle was her answer.

"No, are you?" a disembodied voice said.

"No."

A shuffling sound indicated that the owner of the voice was moving. In the darkness, the sound got closer. Emily pulled her legs closer to her body. She was scanning the room hard looking for anyone who might be there, but couldn't see anyone.

Suddenly a flash of lightning lit up the sky illuminating the room for just a moment. Emily caught sight of something that terrified her. A dark form moving in her direction.

"Eek!" she screamed.

"Sshhh, ya don want dose men ta come in here now do ya?"

A hand reached out of the darkness and gently touched her hand. Emily immediately jerked it back.

"Who are you?" she asked, a tremor in her voice.

"Name's Mercy."

Another flash of lightning showed Emily that a girl about her own age had crept over and was now sitting on her knees in front of her. Emily was completely speechless as she looked into the face of a girl whose skin was so dark, she was almost impossible to see in the poorly lit stall.

"I figgered since we's in this stall together dat we might as well git ta know each other," said the black girl.

"Where did you come from?" Emily asked her, still cowering in the corner. "You weren't in here earlier when I came in. You must be a ghost."

"I's in here da whole time. Ya just didn't see me. I's sittin' in dat corner when ya come in."

"How come I didn't see you then?"

"I's guessin' cause you wasn't lookin' very hard."

"Who are you?" Emily asked, relaxing just a little.

"I tole you already. My name's Mercy. What's your name?"

"Emily. Emily Dunn."

"Well, it's nice ta meet ya, Emily Dunn."

Mercy reached out her hand to shake Emily's. Emily hesitated for a moment, but then gently took Mercy's hand in hers and shook it.

"Do ya mind iffn we sit kinda close? It's awful chilly in here with da rain and all. Mebbe we would be warmer iffn we sits close together."

"I suppose it's ok," Emily said. She shifted her position enough to allow Mercy sit down beside her.

"Where's ya from?" Mercy asked her.

"Pennsylvania. You?"

"Well, I's originally from South Carolina, but I's nabbed from Ohio."

"Nabbed?"

"Yeah, dat means where I's taken from. Ya see, my mama was a slave in South Carolina, but when I's a baby, she 'scaped to Ohio. When dese men found out I's a slave child, dey nabbed me from my mama while we's out pickin' veggies in da farmer's field my mama worked at."

"What about your father? Where is he?"

"Don know. He got sold to another slave massa 'fore I's born. I never knowed him."

"That's horrible!"

"Dat's just da way it is for us slaves. What 'bout you?

"My mother died giving birth to me, so my father raised me. I have a nanny who looks after me when my father is away on business."

"How old ya be?" Mercy asked her.

"Thirteen. You?"

"I's thirteen too."

They heard a rustling noise just outside the stall. Suddenly the dim light from a lantern lit up the small space. Mr. Guthrie's face pressed up against the bars on the door.

"You all hush up in there," he said gruffly. "You best get some sleep. You have a long day ahead of you in the morning."

The girls stared at him, but neither said a word. They inched a little closer to each other and grasped each others hand.

"You hear me?" he asked.

"Yes sir," Emily said in a low voice.

"Yessa," Mercy said louder.

"Good, now get to sleep." he said, turning away from the door and taking the light with him.

The girls sat in the dark, listening for any further noise outside the stall. Everyone in the barn seemed to be asleep, except for the two of them. Outside, the storm continued to rage on.

"How many other girls are here," Emily asked Mercy in a very low whisper.

"I don know 'xactly. Las' time I counted, I's guessing dere were 'bout 10 of us."

"Where did they all come from?"

"We's all been nabbed from da North. I don know none of ta other girls though. I's da only blackie here and none of da other girls wants anyfin' ta do wit me."

"All the other girls are white? Like me?" Emily asked.

"Yep. I's guessin there ain't many blackies in da North, so all dey could git was white 'uns."

"Do you know where they're taking us?"

"I heared da men say they's gonna be takin' us to an auction in South Carolina."

"An auction? What does that mean?"

"It mean they gonna put us up on a auction block and rich plantation owners gonna bid on us. Whoever bids da highest gits ya."

"What happens then?" Emily asked, starting to feel sick to her stomach. It felt like butterflies were dancing around in her belly.

"Den ya go be a slave to dem at their plantation. They make ya do all sorts a things. Wash da clothes, do da ironing, make da dinners, clean da house. Ya name it, ya do it."

"That sounds horrible."

"It's better than workin in da fields. Which I s'ppose is sumpin dey could make ya do too."

"I don't want to be a slave. I don't want to work in someone's house or in their fields," Emily said.

"Well, ya ain't gonna has a choice. Iffn ya don do what dey tell ya, dey'll whip ya."

This was sounding worse and worse. Emily's head swam with images of scrubbing floors and cleaning dishes. She had never done any household chores before. Olive always did them. Would she even know how?

"Emily?" Mercy asked.

"Yes?"

"Ya wanna be my friend?"

"Sure. I'll be your friend."

She actually meant it too. There was something about Mercy that made Emily feel connected to her in some way. She didn't know the girl well, but she knew she really liked her and somewhere deep down inside, she trusted her too.

They cuddled up together in the corner of the stall and eventually, they both drifted off to sleep.

CHAPTER 3

The storm passed sometime during the night. Rays of sunlight streamed in through the holes in the roof casting beams of dust-filled light across the tiny stall.

Emily gently shook Mercy's shoulder to wake her.

It was still early morning. No sound was coming from outside the stall, so Emily assumed everyone else was still asleep.

Mercy roused from her place next to Emily and sat up, rubbing her eyes and giving a huge yawn.

"Good mornin'," Mercy said.

"Good morning to you too," Emily replied.

"It don sound like no one's up yet."

"No, it doesn't. I'm sorry I woke you up so early."

"It's ok. I's surprised da men ain't up yet. We usually gits an early start ever' morning."

"They must have drank themselves into a stupor last night."

"What's a 'stupor'?" Mercy asked her.

"My father said it means when someone drinks so much they can't wake up properly in the morning."

"Oh, well I seen da men do dat plenty den."

"What's going to happen this morning when they do get up?"

"Dey's gonna give us some dry bread and water, den dey gonna slap chains 'round our legs."

"What? Why?" Emily asked, horrified. She started getting that queasy feeling in the pit of her stomach again.

"Dat's how dey keeps us from runnin' away from dem. Dey chain us up and den we gots to walk till we meets up wit another wagon dat will take us to da next stoppin' place."

"How far will we have to walk?"

"Depends," Mercy said, shrugging her shoulders. "Sometimes it only a few miles, sometimes it all day."

Emily was getting ready to ask more questions when she heard the men moving around outside the stall.

Suddenly, the whole barn seemed to come alive. Loud talking and laughing drifted in to them from the aisle as the men were getting breakfast ready. Emily thought she heard girl's voices coming from the other end of the barn.

Mr. Guthrie appeared in front of their stall and unlocked the door. He sauntered in with a smug look on his face.

"Breakfast," he said, as he dropped a couple slices of bread on the floor in front of them. He set a cup of water down between them as well. "Eat up girls. That's all you're getting till supper."

He laughed as he walked back out of the stall, sliding the door closed behind him and locking it.

Emily stared at the bread at her feet and the single cup of water that she and Mercy were to share.

"Ya better git to it," Mercy said, grabbing up some of the bread. "Dey don give us much time ta eat."

Emily picked up a slice of the hard, dry bread and brought it up to her nose and sniffed it. It smelled like bread, but she had never eaten any bread that was this hard before. She looked over at Mercy and watched her rip off a chunk with her front teeth.

Emily placed her teeth over a corner of the bread and bit down on it. It tasted a little stale, but she managed to bite off a piece and chew it. She washed down the bite with a swallow of lukewarm water.

After several bites and a couple of gulps of water, Emily laid aside the bread. She just couldn't eat anymore. Her stomach was in knots and she kept having a hard time breathing.

She knew she was having an anxiety attack. She had had one before when she was asked to perform in a play at Christmastime in front of the whole church. She had gotten so nervous that she ended up unable to perform in the play. She felt even worse now.

Mercy finished her bread and drank the last of the water. When she realized that Emily hadn't finished her bread, she asked if she could have it.

"Of course," Emily said. "No sense in it going to waste."

Just as they finished with their breakfast, Mr. Guthrie came back to the stall.

"Alright girls, let's go," he said as he slid the door open. "Mercy, you know the drill. Make sure Emily does too."

Mercy grabbed Emily's hand and led her out into the aisle between the stalls.

A long chain with manacles about every four feet was stretched out along the floor. Emily saw several girls emerge from a stall farther down from where she and Mercy had been. Each girl stepped up to a manacle and waited beside it while one of the men went along and clasped one around each girl's right ankle.

Mercy stepped up to one and motioned for Emily to step up to the one in front of her. Emily quickly got in place as the man made his way up to them.

The manacle was snapped around Emily's ankle and locked in place. The metal was heavy and cold. She could feel the weight of it dragging down on her leg.

She glanced back at Mercy. Mercy just nodded to her and laid her hand on her shoulder. Emily grasped her hand and squeezed. She was terrified and didn't know what to expect, but with Mercy behind her, she didn't feel so alone.

Mr. Guthrie picked up the chain at the end closest to Emily. He gave it a hard yank which caused all the girls right legs to be jerked forward.

"Now that I have your attention, we're going to go over a few rules before we head out," he said. "First of all, no lagging. If you lag, you will be drug along by your ankle. Second of all, no crying, no yelling, no screaming and no talking. If you're caught doing any of that, you'll be gagged and whipped. Third of all, no trying to escape. If you're caught even attempting to, you'll be shot dead. You got it?"

'Yes sir' echoed up and down the line as each girl responded. Emily mouthed the words, but the sound didn't quite reach her lips. She was trembling from head to toe and was afraid her stomach would heave up the small bit of bread she had eaten.

"Fine. Let's go," Mr. Guthrie said, pulling on the chain.

The line of girls began walking out of the barn. Mr. Guthrie was in the lead, holding the chain all the girls were attached to, while the men took up spots along side the girls and one followed from behind.

Emily had taken a quick head count of the men as they were being chained up and had counted five of them. Yesterday when she had arrived, it seemed like there were more than that, but she was thankful she had been wrong. Five was plenty. She noticed that a couple of them kept looking at her and watching her. It made her feel uncomfortable, but she tried to brush it off.

As they set off across the pasture, the ground was mushy and soft from the previous night's rain.

Mud stuck to Emily's boots and made walking somewhat difficult. She remembered what Mr. Guthrie had said about anyone lagging, so she did her best to keep up the pace.

When they were being chained, she had noticed that Mercy didn't have any boots or stockings on her feet. She had also noticed that Mercy wore a very drab, brownish colored sackcloth dress. It was no wonder she hadn't noticed her in the stall when she first went in. Mercy had blended into the wooden walls and shadowy corner so well, it would have been very difficult for anyone to have seen her there.

Emily looked down at her own brightly colored, floral dress, her dirty stockings and her now, mud caked boots and sighed. Father would be aghast at how filthy she was. Her hair, which was usually pulled back in a neat little bow, was now ratted and messed up. She could only imagine the tangles. Her father always said that her hair was her glory. He said it was just like her mother's. She could feel the weight of it hanging down her back. A few strands of the long, waist length curls hung over her shoulders and seemed to stick to her neck and face.

It had been a couple of days since she had enjoyed a hot bath. Mr. Cordell had insisted that she stay clean and neat on the way down and had ordered a bath for her every other night they stayed at an inn. How she wished for a long, hot bath now.

They got to the edge of the pasture where woods grew thick and tall beyond the fence. There was a break in the fence that Mr. Guthrie led them through. Emily noticed he seemed to know exactly where he was going and wondered how many times he had made this journey and how many girls had been kidnapped and brought through here.

They negotiated their way through the woods for a couple of hours. Emily's feet were beginning to ache and sweat was running down her face and neck. She was starting to get really thirsty too.

The woods were shaded by the tall, thickly leafed trees, but the heat rising up from the ground was sweltering. Emily could tell that everyone was starting to feel uncomfortable. Even Mr. Guthrie. He repeatedly pulled a handkerchief from his pocket and sopped up the sweat from his forehead.

They marched on for another half hour when the trees began to thin out slightly and the sound of a river could be heard just up ahead. Emily's spirits rose at the thought of the cool water. She hoped they would be allowed to stop and get a drink.

Her wish was granted when Mr. Guthrie called over his shoulder. "We're gonna take a break here," he said.

They emerged from the woods onto a small river bank. Mr. Guthrie dropped the chain and lunged headlong into the water. The other men did the same, not even bothering to remove their clothes.

The girls all stood on the bank and watched as the men swam around and drank from the river.

Emily started to move forward when Mercy grabbed her shoulder.

"No, Emily," she said. "We's ta wait here til dey git done."

"Why?" Emily asked. "Aren't we allowed to get a drink?"

"Dey gits ta go first. When dey's done, den dey allows us ta go in."

Emily looked back at the men in the water and felt a deep anger and bitterness toward them. It just wasn't fair. She was just as tired and thirsty as they were.

She sat down on the bank and glared at the men. The other girls all took seats as well and began chatting to one another.

One of the girls looked at Emily and whispered something to the other girls. Emily tried to hear what she said, but wasn't close enough to hear her.

Suddenly the eyes of all the other girls fell on her. She looked at them expectantly, waiting to hear what they were going to say.

"Hey you," one of the girls called to her. "What's your name?"

Mercy leaned in to her and whispered softly in her ear so the other girls wouldn't hear her.

"Don ya go payin' no mind to dem. Dey's not da nicest girls."

Emily looked from Mercy to the girl who had called out to her. She choose to ignore the girl and looked back out at the river.

"Hey, I'm talking to you, girl," the girl called again. "What's your name?"

"Emily," Emily said, not looking at the girl.

"Well, Emily, you don't want to go consorting with the wrong kind."

"What do you mean?" Emily asked, looking over at her with a scowl on her face.

"You don't want to be making friends with a darkie."

Emily caught the meaning of the girls words and turned to look her straight in the face.

"You better watch what you say about my friend."

"Your friend? Did you just hear what I said? You don't want to go mixing with her kind."

Emily got to her feet and looked down at the girl who was still a few feet away. "Seems to me, her kind is the kind I *do* want to consort with. If being kind is so wrong, then I would prefer to be wrong. It's you I don't think I want to consort with."

The other girl jumped up and lunged at Emily. She grabbed a fistful of her hair and tackled her to the ground. Emily was so surprised by the attack, that she didn't know what to do, so she curled up in a ball and screamed.

Suddenly, the girl was jerked off of her and tossed to the ground. Emily sat up and saw one of the men looming over her.

"We got a problem here?" he asked gruffly.

The other girl staggered to her feet and pointed at Emily. "She started it!"

The man looked from Emily to the other girl and started laughing. "Looks like we might have a cat fight on our hands, boys."

The other men, including Mr. Guthrie burst out laughing.

Emily looked at Mercy to see what her reaction was. Mercy's eye were wide and her mouth hung open. Emily was getting ready to ask her what was wrong, when the man leaned down and unlocked the manacle from around her ankle. He walked over and did the same to the other girl.

He came back to Emily and snatched her up so quickly around the waist, she didn't have time to react. He then grabbed the other girl up in the same fashion and walked to the edge of the river. In one swift movement he hurled Emily and the other girl into the water.

Emily hit the water, landing on her stomach. She quickly gained her feet, but had swallowed a mouthful of water and was gasping for breath.

"If you two want to fight, then get to it," said the man who had thrown them in.

Emily looked over at the other girl, who had also gained her feet, and waited to see what the girl would do. To Emily's surprise and horror, the girl lunged at her again. This time Emily saw it coming and moved out of the way. The other girl landed face first into the water.

The girl surfaced and made a growling noise in her throat and moved menacingly toward Emily again. Emily swung back her hand and slapped the girl hard across the face.

"Stop that now!" she demanded. "That's no way for a lady to act!"

The other girl was so dumbfounded by what Emily had done that she just stood there staring at her.

The men on the bank roared with laughter until Mr. Guthrie spoke up. "Alright, enough," he bellowed. "Get the other girls in the water. They're starting to stink and need a good bathing as well."

All the girls were allowed to get into the water after removing their outerwear. Dressed only in their chemises and drawers, they waded into the water. Mercy made her way to Emily's side and clasped her hand.

"Thanks for stickin' up fer me. No one's ever done dat before."

Emily squeezed her hand. "Of course I stuck up for you. You're my friend."

They played in the water and scrubbed as much mud and grime off of themselves as they could before the men called them back to the bank.

Chained up again, Emily and Mercy were now in the back of the line. Emily was glad to be in the back. That way she could watch what the other girls were doing instead of being the one who was watched.

They had crossed the river by way of a swinging rope bridge that was farther down the river from where they had stopped to swim. Crossing the bridge was a new experience for Emily. One she didn't care to repeat. The bridge sagged and swayed with each step she took and she feared she would end up in the river again, but she had made it to the other side safely and without incident.

Daylight was waning as they continued to make their way through the woods.

Mr. Guthrie stopped them when they reached a small clearing. Emily looked around and noticed it had a campfire in the middle of it. Dried wood and small kindling was stacked next to it.

One of the men set to work building a fire while the other men began unchaining the girls.

Emily's dress was almost dry by this point, but her stockings and boots were still wet. Each time she took a step, her leather boots squeaked and squished. She would be glad to remove them and hoped they would dry by morning.

As the girls were released from their manacles, they each found a place to sit down. Emily and Mercy chose a spot a short distance from the other girls.

Once seated, Emily quickly removed her boots and pulled off her stockings. She set them down on the ground next to her. She noticed her toes were wrinkly from being wet for so long. She wriggled them around letting air move between them.

"I's guessin' we gonna be stayin' here for da night," Mercy said.

"Here? Outside? In the dark? On the ground?" Emily asked. She looked around her and shivered.

"We don always gits a barn ta stay in. Sometimes we jus has ta sleep on da ground."

"What about animals?"

"Da fire'll keep dem away. Don worry. Da men has guns too."

At the mention of guns, Emily's head snapped up and she looked over at the men. Another shiver ran up her spine.

Once the fire was lit, a large pot was placed on top of it. Emily watched one of the men pull something out of a pack he was carrying and dump it into the pot.

"What is that?" she asked Mercy.

"It's beans."

"Is that our dinner?"

"Yup."

"Are they good?"

"Nope."

Emily could smell the beans heating up. They didn't smell like Olive's beans. These smelled like they were already burnt.

The men filled bowls with the hot mixture and set one bowl down between two girls. Each man had his own bowl.

"We's s'posed ta share a bowl," Mercy told Emily.

"There isn't enough to share," Emily said, examining the contents of the bowl.

"We jus gotta make do."

Mercy reached into the bowl with her fingers and pulled out a helping of beans and stuffed it into her mouth. "Ya git used to it," she said, with her mouth full.

Emily slowly dipped her fingers into the bowl and pulled out a finger full of beans and lifted it to her mouth. She hesitated at the burnt smell, but since she hadn't eaten all her bread at breakfast, her stomach was empty, so she quickly shoved the beans into her mouth.

They finished their bowl and licked their fingers clean. It wasn't nearly enough to fill their bellies, but they were thankful for what they did get.

The men walked around and collected the bowls from the girls. Emily realized they didn't bother to clean them before stuffing them back into the pack.

Light was fading fast as night moved in.

Mr. Guthrie threw a couple more logs onto the fire then settled back on his elbows on the ground next to it. He stretched out his legs and crossed them. Snapping his fingers at the men, he pointed to the girls.

The men jumped up and began clamping the manacles around the girls ankles, then securely fastened the end of the chain around a tree, locking it into place.

Mercy sat down with her back against the tree they were sitting under. Emily scooted over next to her. They leaned on each other as they watched the men go about their nightly chores before settling down next to the fire with Mr. Guthrie.

"I suppose it's useless to complain that they all get to sleep near the fire to stay warm while we have to sit under these trees, several feet away."

"Yup," Mercy murmured.

"Well, at least we have each other to help us stay warm."

"Yup."

"Mercy, are you alright?"

"'Course I is. I's jus plumb wore out."

"Yeah, me too."

"Goes ta sleep now, Emily. We's got another long day 'head of us tomorrie."

Emily realized that Mercy was already nodding off. She wished she could drop off that easily, but she was still new to all of this. Her mind raced with a thousand questions. None of which she would get answers to.

She leaned her head on Mercy's shoulder and listened to the night noises around her.

The wind was gently blowing through the treetops causing a soft whooshing sound. She could hear the shuffling of small woodland animals running around gathering up their dinner.

After a short time, the men's snoring filled the clearing, and therefore, any hope of falling asleep. She was not used to sleeping outdoors. She was not used to hearing snoring. She was not used to sleeping on the hard ground. So she sat awake well into the early hours of the morning.

Around dawn, she finally drifted off into a fitful sleep.

CHAPTER 4

"Emily! Emily wake up!"

"Ummm, what?"

Emily was vaguely aware of Mercy shaking her shoulder. She slowly opened her eyes and glanced around. Everyone was awake and bustling about the camp.

"It's morning already?" Emily asked, sitting up and rubbing her eyes.

"Yup, yous da only one still sleepin'."

"I couldn't sleep. I was awake all night."

"Well, sumpins up. Da men been hurryin' 'round da camp all mornin. I heared one of dem say someone's a comin' ta git us. I's hopin' it's a wagon. My legs still hurt from all dat walkin' we dun yesterday."

"Yeah, my legs are tired too."

Emily watched as one of the men put the fire out that was still burning from the night before. A couple of the others stacked more wood next to the fire pit. Emily knew they were preparing for the next bunch of girls that would be brought through this way. She felt a tug on her heart for the girls who would endure the same fate as her.

"Are we going to get breakfast this morning?" Emily asked.

"Don look like it," Mercy said.

Mr. Guthrie came over to where all the girls were still chained up. Unlocking the chain from the tree, he gave it a good shake.

"Get up, girlies," he said, gruffly. "We've got a bit of a hike today to get to the meeting spot. Dust yourselves off and let's go."

"Sir," Emily asked, timidly. "Who are we meeting?"

Mr. Guthrie just stared at her for a moment. At first, Emily didn't think he was going to answer her, but he leaned down to look her directly in the face and spat on the ground in front of her.

"We're meeting up with a wagon just yonder through the woods over there. Looks like you'll get a break from walking for awhile. But don't get too happy about it. It'll just get us to our destination a bit faster, which means I'll get rid of you whiny little brats that much sooner."

He turned his back toward the girls and cocked one of his legs up into the air. He then farted loudly in their direction. Laughing, he strolled off into the woods.

"That man is just foul," Emily said, waving her hand in front of her face.

"He sho is," Mercy said.

Emily quickly put her stockings and boots back on, which had actually dried out overnight. She glanced down at Mercy's bare feet and felt ashamed that she had boots to wear and Mercy had none.

Quickly slipping her boots back off, she handed them to Mercy.

"What ya doin'?" Mercy asked her.

"You don't have any boots, so I am giving you mine."

"No ma'am. Tank ya, but I's don wear dem old uncomfortable tings. My mama bought me a pair when I's younger and dey hurt my feet sumpin awful. I jus prefer my bare feet."

Emily stared dumbfounded at her.

"Don look at me like dat. I's much happier wifout 'em."

Emily slipped her boots back on, shaking her head. How could walking barefoot through the woods be more comfortable than with boots? Her feet would be all cut up and sore if she went barefoot. She glanced down the line of girls and realized that several of them didn't have boots or shoes of any kind. She wriggled her toes inside her boots and realized that her feet were actually rather sore. Maybe she should go barefoot after all. The other girls didn't seem to complain about their feet hurting, so maybe it was more comfortable to go barefoot after all.

About that time, Mr. Guthrie sauntered back out of the woods. He picked up the end of the chain that the girls were all manacled to. Without so much as a word, he began walking down a narrow path that disappeared into the woods, dragging the girls behind him.

Once again, Emily and Mercy were chained at the front of the line.

The trail they were following was slightly overgrown and very narrow in spots. Emily realized that if someone was to lie down in the overgrowth just off the path, no one would be able to see them. An idea was taking shape in her mind. She needed to talk to Mercy.

They trudged along for about an hour, when a horse's neighing reached them through the dense woods. Emily looked around Mr. Guthrie's bulk to see if she could get a glimpse of what was up ahead. She caught sight of a long wagon being pulled by four horses.

They broke through the trees and came out onto a dirt road that stretched on out of sight in both directions.

The road was narrow, with deep ruts. It was still muddy from the rains, but since they weren't going to be walking, Emily supposed it didn't matter. The horses hooves were covered in mud, but they didn't seem to mind.

Two big, burly men sat on the seat in the front of the wagon, while another, smaller man, was pulling large blankets out of the back and throwing them onto the ground.

Mr. Guthrie led the girls to the back of the wagon and stopped. The man throwing out the blankets spoke to him in a low voice. Emily tried, but wasn't able to hear what he said.

Suddenly, both men turned toward Emily and looked her up and down. Heat rose in her cheeks as she took a step backwards.

"Oh yeah, she'll bring you a good price alright. She sure is a fine looking one," the man talking to Mr. Guthrie said.

Mr. Guthrie just nodded with a sickeningly large smile on his face.

"Time to get loaded up," Mr. Guthrie said.

He called for his men to start unlocking the girls from their chains. One by one, he lifted them into the wagon.

"Now get on back in there. Move all the way to the back," he instructed them.

Emily and Mercy made their way to a corner and sat down. The other girls all moved back toward them and sat down wherever they could find a seat.

Mr. Guthrie jumped up into the wagon and stood over them, looking down at each girl in turn. "Most of you know how this goes by now, but for those of you who are new to this, you'll stay laying down in your spot and keep your mouth closed. You'll be covered up with those blankets to keep

anyone from seeing you. If you move around or make any noise, I'll strangle you myself. Got it?"

"Yes sir," was mumbled by every girl.

Mr. Guthrie's men began tossing the blankets up into the wagon. He threw a blanket back to Emily and Mercy.

"Lay down and cover yourselves up completely," he said.

He threw the rest of the blankets to the other girls, instructing them to do the same thing.

Once all the girls were completely covered by the blankets, Mr. Guthrie and his men climbed in and took seats in the back of the wagon.

It was a bit cramped, but Emily figured it was still better than walking.

She was laying next to Mercy with their heads only inches apart.

"I have something I want to talk to you about," she whispered into Mercy's ear.

"Ssshhh, we's not s'posed to talk," Mercy said.

"I know, but I'll just whisper it in your ear."

"Ok den, goes ahead."

"I think I know of a way we can escape."

"Wha? Ya don los' ya mind?" Mercy asked.

"No, listen," Emily said. "The manacle around my ankle is kind of loose. I noticed it last night when I took my boots off. I think if we try hard enough, we can pull our feet out when they aren't looking and make a run for."

"No ma'am. Dey shoot us dead iffn we's ta even try it."

"Not if they don't know we did. I have a plan."

Emily quietly told Mercy her plan.

"Ya know, dat might jus work," Mercy said, mulling it over in her mind.

"I say we give it a shot. I don't want to become a slave and the only way to make sure we don't is to get away. What do you say? Should we go for it?"

Mercy was quiet for several minutes. Emily had begun to think that she had fallen asleep.

Finally Mercy whispered in Emily's ear. "Yeah, I tink it's worf a try."

"Good," said Emily. "The next opportunity that comes, we go for it."

Excitement raced through Emily as she reached down and grabbed Mercy's hand and squeezed it.

The wagon took off with a sudden jolt. Emily could hear the men snapping the reins across the horses backs and calling 'giddy-up'. The clippity clop of the horse's hooves sounded rhythmic as they trotted down the road.

The girls were jostled around under their blankets, but every one of them was thankful for the ride. It sure beat walking.

Emily's mind was a whirlwind of ideas on exactly how they would escape.

After several hours in the back of the wagon, she had it totally planned out.

Now to wait for the right time.

CHAPTER 5

It was several days before Emily and Mercy could even consider their escape.

They traveled by wagon for days. The only time they would stop was at night when they would find a place to camp that was hidden from any passersby.

They were eventually dropped off in a small, dusty town in the middle of nowhere, where no one seemed to notice that the men had several girls locked up in chains.

Emily had tried to get the attention of a man they passed on the street, but he purposely looked the other way and walked on past them.

Emily knew they must be deep in the South now. They were used to slavery down here, so no one took any notice of them.

They passed through the town and eventually traveled down a lonely dirt road that seemed to go nowhere.

Food had been sparse over the last few days and Emily's stomach had began to get a deep ache in it. She was dirty. Her dress was torn in several places and her stockings had holes all through them. Her boots were worn and scuffed. Her long, beautiful hair was matted in knots. She had stopped trying to run her fingers through it because all she did was pull out strands and make her scalp hurt. She was miserable and all she wanted to do was cry.

She began dragging her feet and kicking up dust as she walked.

Mr. Guthrie jerked on the chain and gave her a scathing look.

"I'll drag you girl, if you don't pick up the pace," he said, nastily.

She merely nodded at him, but was careful from then on not to drag her feet anymore.

She had learned over the course of the trip, that Mr. Guthrie was good on his threats. One of the other girls had tripped and landed on her hands and knees. Mr. Guthrie had just jerked on the chain and kept walking. The girl was drug several yards before she could regain her feet and walk again. Later that evening, Emily saw that her hands and knees were scraped up pretty bad. She decided right then, that she would not give Mr. Guthrie any reason to do the same to her.

The day wore on. The sun was relentless and the humidity was draining all the energy out of her. Dust was caked on her face and her throat felt parched.

Soon, they came to a place where the road narrowed even more and woods grew up on either side. The tree's branches began to form a canopy over the road and offered some much needed shade.

Just a short distance up the road, Mr. Guthrie turned into the woods. The slight drop in temperature from the shade of the trees was a relief to Emily.

The woods here were closely compacted. Making their way through them was difficult as they had to climb over fallen logs, step around large stones and walk through bushes that were thorny.

Finally, they stopped near a fast flowing stream.

Emily sat on the bank after getting her drink from the cool, clean water. Mercy plopped down next to her.

"It's almos' time," she said quietly to Emily. "I feels it in my bones."

"Me too," Emily said. She knew once they had entered the woods that the opportunity to try to escape was close at hand. These woods were denser than the last ones they had stayed at and as she scanned her surroundings, she knew they could make their escape soon.

To their surprise, Mr. Guthrie announced that they would be making camp there for the night. *What a stroke of luck*, thought Emily. They were surrounded by thick woods and now they would have the sound of the stream to cover any noise they might make. She almost squealed out loud at their good fortune, but caught herself just in time. She didn't want to do anything that might make Mr. Guthrie or his men think she was up to something.

She moved back away from the bank to sit under a tree. She settled herself down and looked carefully around at her surroundings. She didn't want to mess this up, so she took note of the direction they had come from and the direction they were headed in. She figured it was best not to go back the way they had come in case they ran into another group of men bringing some more girls down to the south. She didn't want to go in the direction they were headed in because the men would just end up catching up to them. So considering her options, she decided it was best to go off to the right of the campsite.

Since they were not chained up yet, Emily went and grabbed Mercy by the hand and led her to the side of the makeshift campsite that they would make their escape from.

Sitting down under a tree again, she leaned in and whispered to Mercy. "We'll make our escape tonight."

Mercy simply gave a quick nod and pretended to be looking at her feet.

One of the men built a fire and tossed on another bunch of beans. When their meal was dropped in front of them, Emily and Mercy wolfed down their meager dinner then leaned back against the tree.

They had both lost a considerable amount of weight. The lack of proper food and the long walks had taken their toll. Emily knew they would have no problem pulling their legs out of the shackles now. There wasn't much meat left on them.

Night wore on and once again, the men came over and clamped the manacles back around their ankles. Even though all the girls were only about four feet apart, they tried to keep as much distance between themselves as possible. Except Emily and Mercy. The men didn't seem to pay any attention to how close they sat since they had been doing this from the first night they were together. Emily gave a quick prayer of thanks to God for that.

Finally, darkness covered the woods. The inky blackness made it hard to see the hand in front of your face. The only light came from the fire and it had burned down to embers. They didn't need it for warmth since it was so hot outside, but they kept it going to keep animals out of the camp.

After what felt like hours, all the men had settled down and the only noise was the sound of the gurgling stream.

After making sure the other girls were asleep, Emily leaned close to Mercy and whispered in her ear. "It's time. Are you ready?"

"Yup."

Emily had laid out the plan for Mercy over the long days of riding in the wagon. They knew they could not just slip out of their chains and take off running. Someone would notice they were gone. The men did nightly checks to make sure the girls were still there. So Emily came up with the idea of removing their dresses and laying them on the ground by the chains as if they were still in them. That way, when the men walked by, they would see the dresses and believe the girls were still there.

After a final check to make sure everyone else was still asleep, Emily and Mercy quickly, but quietly, pulled their skinny legs out of the manacles. Then they slipped off their dresses and laid them out on the ground next to the manacles as quietly as they could. They were careful to arrange them to look like someone was still in them. Emily even removed her boots and stockings and set them next to the tree where they could be spotted.

Wearing only their chemises and drawers, they stealthily crept off into the woods and the darkness beyond.

They paused every now and then to listen to see if they heard shouts or cries coming from the camp, but no noise was heard.

They crept on quietly till dawn began to break across the sky.

They had no idea where they were, but they knew they had to find a place to hide. Once the men realized they were gone, they would come looking for them.

The woods thinned out and eventually opened up into a large field. Tall grass grew in rows that reached way over their heads. Emily didn't know what kind of grass it was, but she knew it would offer them cover as they made their way through it. Even though she couldn't see where it went, she knew it had to eventually come out to somewhere.

"We'll have cover as we cross the field," she told Mercy.

"Good, cuz we's not outta danger yet," Mercy told her, as she started off into the tall grass.

Emily followed her and soon they were completely hidden from view from anyone who might be passing by the field.

The tall rows of grass were easy to move through. The ground under foot was hard and compact.

"Emily grabbed Mercy's hand and laughed.

"It worked! We did it! Now we just have to figure out how to get home!"

"Don go gittin' all excited yet. We don even know where we is."

Emily didn't let Mercy's caution get her down. She was so happy that they were free and she wasn't going to let a little thing like not knowing where they were ruin her mood. She began to sing a song that Olive had taught her about a butterfly being free.

Mercy quickly jerked her to a stop. "Quiet now, Em. We's not safe yet."

Emily looked at Mercy and realized by the look on her face that she was scared. She stopped singing at once.

"I'm sorry, Mercy," she said. "I guess it would be best if we kept quiet and didn't make any noise."

"Yup. We don know if dem men are out lookin' fer us yet or not, but iffn dey is, we don want dem findin' us."

Emily realized the wisdom of Mercy's words. A solemn mood fell over her as she realized they were a long way from being free yet.

CHAPTER 6

Up ahead, Emily could see they were coming to the end of the tall grass. She slowed her pace when she realized it opened up into a yard.

Stopping just before they stepped out into the yard, she slowly poked her head out of the grass and looked around.

A weathered old house stood in the middle of a yard that was almost completely devoid of grass, except for a few small patches here and there. A clothesline, full of clothes, stretched from the side of the house to an old tree several yards away.

"You think anyone is home?" Emily asked Mercy in a low whisper.

"Don know. Les jus watch da place fer a moment and see iffn anyone comes out."

They watched the house for several minutes, but no one seemed to be home.

"Should we go up to the house and see if anyone's home?" Emily asked.

"What's ya gonna say ta dem? Dey gonna knows we's runaways. We ain't even got any proper clothes."

Emily looked at the clothesline and then down at her chemise and drawers.

"I have an idea."

"What ya tinkin'?"

"If no one is home, we could borrow some of those clothes off the clothesline."

"Borrah? Ya mean steal dem. Iffn we's ta take dem clothes, I's not plannin' on bringin' dem back!"

"Well, ok. I guess we would be stealing them, but we can't keep running around in our under clothes, now can we?"

"No, I's guessin' not."

They waited for a few more minutes, then Emily stepped out of the grass and into the yard. She paused to see if anyone would come out of the house, but no one did.

She took several steps into the yard before she realized that Mercy wasn't behind her. She turned back toward her and motioned with her arm for Mercy to join her.

Mercy hesitated a moment, then slowly joined Emily in the yard.

"I's scared, Em."

"Why? Do you see someone?"

"No, dat's why I's scared. Where'd dey go? What if dey comes back while we's stealin' dere clothes?"

"Then we run back into the grass."

Mercy nervously glanced around, but followed Emily to the clothesline. There were several pairs of men's trousers and a few women's dresses, along with some undergarments and a sheet set. Emily perused the dresses and chose a powder blue one. Mercy just stood there staring at the house.

"Mercy, pick a dress and let's go," Emily whispered to her urgently.

Mercy glanced at the clothes, but continued to stare at the house.

"I tink someone is here. I hears sumpin."

Emily quickly grabbed another dress off the line and shoved it into Mercy's hands.

"There's a hole under the porch. Let's crawl under there and wait."

Grabbing Mercy by the hand, she ran toward the house. When they reached the porch, she quickly dropped to her hands and knees and crawled under it.

It wasn't a big porch, so the space wasn't that big, but it offered them enough room to squirm into their new dresses.

Emily watched as Mercy slid the calico dress she had grabbed for her, over her head. She couldn't help but stare at the color of Mercy's skin. She had never seen skin so dark or beautiful before.

"You have such beautiful skin, Mercy," she said in awe.

Mercy stopped tugging on the dress and just stared at Emily.

"No I don," she said. The look on her face was one of total disbelief.

"What do you mean? Yes, you do. It's so dark and smooth. It reminds me of the dark chocolate cake Olive used to bake."

"Well, you's so white, I can almost see tru ya."

Emily realized that Mercy seemed angry.

"Why are you mad?"

"Ya sittin' over dere tellin' me I has beautiful skin. What ya tinkin'? My skin's not purty at all. Iffn it was, den whys all da white folk hate me so much?"

"Well…," Emily stammered, trying to come up with an answer to Mercy's question. "Because they're stupid, that's why! I'm white and I don't hate you! And I think you're beautiful."

"You's jus crazy."

Emily reached out and touched Mercy's face with her fingertips. She ran her finger across her cheek, then reached up and squeezed one of the curls on Mercy's head.

"You have really interesting hair too. It feels like wool."

"Yup, yous crazy," Mercy said, shaking her head. She reached over and touched Emily's face in the same way Emily had touched hers.

"Yo skin feels jus like mine."

"Of course it does. You thought it would feel different?"

Mercy grabbed a strand of Emily's hair and ran it through her fingers.

"You's hair is so soft. Ya have awful beautiful hair."

"Thank you," Emily said. "You shouldn't ever let anyone tell you you aren't beautiful, cause you are."

Mercy just shook her head again and chuckled. "You's jus crazy."

Emily slipped the powder blue dress that she had chosen over her head and realized it was too big. She looked over at Mercy and saw that hers too, was too big.

"We need to tie these up or we'll trip over them when we walk."

Mercy glanced down at the loose fabric around her waist and then gathered up the hem of the dress. She began looking around on the ground around her.

"What are you looking for?" Emily asked her.

"A rock."

"What for?"

"I's gonna rip da bottom o' dis dress off so's it don drag on da ground."

"So what's the rock for?"

"Dat's what I's gonna rip da dress wif."

Emily started searching the ground for a rock too. She found one and handed it to Mercy. "Will this one do?"

Mercy took the rock and turned it over in her hand, then tossed it away from her. "Nah, it has ta be sharp. Like dis one," she said, picking up a rock and showing it to Emily.

The rock was small and thin and had a rough edge on one side. Mercy gathered up the hem of the dress and began gouging the rock into the fabric. Soon a small tear formed. She stuck her finger into the tear and began ripping the fabric until she had torn a piece of fabric several inches long off the bottom of the dress.

Handing the rock to Emily, she told her to do the same. Emily copied what Mercy had done and managed to remove several inches off the length of her dress as well.

They gathered up the discarded fabric and tied it around their waists so the dresses were snug around their middle.

Satisfied that the dresses fit better now, they examined each other's handwork and giggled.

"Sho is better den runnin' 'round in our knickers," Mercy said.

"Oh yes. That color looks good on you too," Emily said, admiring the way the calico colors looked on Mercy.

"I like dat blue one ya gots too."

Emily looked down at the dress she had on and looked back at Mercy's.

"Want to trade?"

Mercy looked down at her dress and shook her head. "Nah, I likes all da colors in dis one."

Suddenly a warm, sweet smell drifted in under the porch. Emily's stomach immediately began to rumble.

"Where is that delicious smell coming from?"

"I don know, but it sho smells like heaven."

Emily stuck her head out from under the porch and sniffed the air. The aroma seemed to be coming from the side of the house.

"I think we should see what it is."

"Me too," Mercy readily agreed.

They crawled out from under the porch on their bellies. Dusting themselves off, they slowly and cautiously made their way around the side of the house following the direction the smell was coming from.

As they neared a window, Mercy suddenly grabbed Emily's arm and gasped.

"It's a pie coolin' in da winder."

"Oohhhh my. Grab it!" Emily said, pushing Mercy toward the window.

Mercy gingerly approached the window and stood up on her tiptoes to look inside. She didn't see anyone about, so she grabbed the pie and pulled it down for Emily to see.

"What kine do ya tink it is?'

"Who cares, let's just eat it!"

Emily shoved her fingers into the warm pie and pulled out a handful. She quickly shoved it into her mouth.

"Oohhh, it's blackberry!" she said with her mouth full.

Mercy didn't waste any time shoving her fingers into the pie and grabbing up a handful herself. Stuffing it into her mouth, she rolled her eyes back in her head. "It's so good."

They stood under the window and ate till there was no pie left. Mercy looked down at the empty pie plate and sighed. She slid the plate back onto the window ledge.

"I want some more," Emily said.

Mercy looked at her and started laughing.

"What's so funny?" Emily asked her.

"Ya has pie all over ya face," Mercy said between giggles.

Emily looked at Mercy and began to giggle too. "So do you!"

Both girls began to giggle harder until they were laughing out loud.

A low growl sounded right behind them. They swung around and came face to face with a large, scroungy dog.

The dog stood about ten feet from them. He just stood there looking at them, but made no move to come toward them.

"Em, wha do we do?" Mercy asked. There was a tremor in her voice.

"Slowly back up," Emily told her.

Both girls began to slowly step backwards one step at a time, when the dog suddenly took a few steps toward them.

Emily had never encountered a mean dog before and fear overtook her.

"Run, Mercy!" she yelled.

Both girls turned on their heels and began to run as fast as they could toward the front of the house.

They scrambled over a road that crossed the front of the property and into the woods on the other side.

Once in the cover of the trees, they turned around to see if the dog was still chasing them. They could see him standing in the front yard of the house, but he wasn't making any move to come after them.

"Do you think he'll keep coming after us?" Emily asked.

"I don know. Where'd he come from?" Mercy asked.

"I don't know. He came out of nowhere."

They continued walking through the woods for the rest of the day. They weren't sure which direction they were heading in, but they kept moving forward. Emily figured each step they took would get them farther away from the men and closer to home.

Every once in awhile, they would look behind them to find that the dog was still following them at a distance. He never came too close, but he was always there.

As darkness began to fall, the girls started looking for a place to stop for the night. After weeks of traveling with the men who had kidnapped them, sleeping outdoors on the ground wasn't a problem anymore. They just needed to find a comfortable place where they could lay down and get some sleep.

Soon they came upon a small clearing just big enough for the two of them to lie down in.

The ground was covered in ferns and thick blankets of moss. Dense woods surrounded them making it seem dark and eerie, but the canopy of trees overhead allowed a sliver of moonlight to filter through. It wasn't enough to offer much light, but Emily was thankful for what little bit it did provide. It was scary to be all alone in the dark. At least with the men, they had other people around. Now it was just her and Mercy. And the dog.

"We's not gonna be able ta has a fire," Mercy said,

"Why not? We need one to keep the animals away."

"Iffn we's ta light a fire and dem men be out dere lookin' fer us, it'd fer sho give us away."

"Oh, I hadn't thought of that," Emily said, frowning.

She wasn't sure how they would have started a fire anyway. She had never started one before and she was pretty sure Mercy didn't know how to start one either, though she had never asked her.

The girls curled up on the ground together as the night sky darkened to a deep purple. The moss was soft and spongy and offered a much softer bed then the hard ground they were used to sleeping on. The earthy smell of the woods was oddly comforting.

Emily couldn't see the dog, but she knew he was out there. Even though she was afraid of him, she felt a moment of comfort knowing he was close by. If anyone came sneaking around while they were sleeping, the dog would alert them to their presence.

"Mercy?" Emily asked.

"Yeah?" came Mercy's groggy reply.

"Do you think we'll ever make it home?"

"Sho do."

"How do you know?"

"Cause I wants it so bad."

"Well, I want it too, but that doesn't mean it'll happen," Emily said.

"Sho it does. When ya wants sumpin bad enough, ya makes it happen. Dat's what my mama always tole me."

"I hope your mama is right."

"She always right."

Emily pondered Mercy's words. Was it true that if you wanted something bad enough, you could make it happen? She sure hoped so, because she wanted to go home really bad. She missed her father and Olive. She missed all the home cooked meals Olive prepared every evening. She missed her soft, comfortable bed.

Please Lord, let us make it home, she prayed.

She lay in the dark for several moments listening to all the noises around her. Somewhere nearby, an owl hooted softly. A gentle breeze ruffled the leaves of the trees overhead. She thought for a moment that she could even hear the dog snoring.

Sleepiness began to overtake her and she let out a long sigh.

"Good night, Mercy."

"'Night, Em."

Emily snuggled up close against Mercy's back and eventually drifted off to sleep. She dreamed of being back home with her dad and Olive, curled up, safe and warm, in her own bed. A silent tear slid down her cheek.

CHAPTER 7

Emily was rudely awakened by something wet and rubbery sliding across her cheek. She reached up to wipe the slobber from her face when she saw that the dog was standing over her. She sat up quickly and gasped.

At her sudden movement, the dog backed off several feet, then just sat there staring at her.

Mercy rolled over to see what was going on. Her eyes flew open when she saw the dog.

"Did he bite ya?" she asked Emily.

"No, he licked my face."

"Mebbe he was tastin ya ta see iffn ya tasted good."

"Eewww, he left slobber all over my face," Emily said, using the sleeve of her dress to wipe her face.

"Yup, he was tastin ya alright."

Emily stared at the dog for a moment. He just sat there staring back at her.

She noticed he didn't seem so mean now. Why did he growl at them yesterday, then follow them all day without attacking them? Why did he wake her up? Was he really just tasting her to see if she would make a good meal? She didn't think so. He seemed to be watching over them. Maybe he wasn't expecting them to be at that farm yesterday and reacted out of fear. She didn't know a whole lot about dogs since she had never owned one. Her father told her dogs were a lot of work, so he didn't allow her to have one.

She looked back at the dog again and wondered if he was just lonely and scared like she and Mercy were.

Mercy gave a loud yawn and stretched, throwing her arms out to the sides.

"We best git movin' Em. We don want dem men comin' 'cross us sleepin'."

Emily stood up and dusted off her dress. She gazed around the area, but everything seemed calm and quiet.

"Mercy, do you really think those men are still looking for us? I mean, maybe they just decided to go on and not worry about us."

"No, Em. Dat ain't how dem men works. Dey'll keep lookin' till dey find us. We's money to dem and dey don like ta lose money. Dey gonna be right mad dat we outsmarted dem too."

"Well then, I guess we better get going."

They headed off into the woods with the dog following a short distance behind.

They had walked for about three hours when Mercy suddenly came to a halt. She turned to Emily who was right behind her and placing her finger to her lips, indicated for Emily to be quiet.

"What is it?" Emily whispered.

"Lissen," Mercy said. "Do ya hear dat?

Emily strained her ears and from somewhere off in the distance, she thought she could hear singing.

"I hear it. What do we do?"

"I don know. Mebbe it's da men. We needs ta go another way."

"No, wait," Emily said, laying her hand on Mercy's arm. "Listen. It's a woman singing."

The lyrics of *Amazing Grace* sung in a high pitched, angelic voice could be heard floating through the air.

"I think we should go see if she can help us," Emily said.

"Em, I don tink dat's a good idea. What if she ain't a nice woman. What if she gives us back ta dos men?"

Emily considered the question a moment before she answered. "We have to take the chance. If she tries to harm us, we'll just run."

"I don know, Em. I's not wantin' ta get inta any more trouble."

"Come on, Mercy. Let's just go see, ok?"

Mercy reluctantly followed Emily to the edge of the wood line. They could see a tiny cabin sitting in a very small clearing. A tiny garden sat to one side of the house and an older woman was sitting on the front porch in a rocking chair. It looked like she was knitting something. Her singing was much clearer now and Emily was amazed at how beautiful it was. It was almost mesmerizing with it's lilting tones.

Emily stepped out of the woods with Mercy close on her heels.

The woman on the porch stopped her singing and her hands became still as she watched the two girls approach her.

"Well howdy there, girls," she said. She had a suspicious look on her face, but it was more of confusion than fear.

"Hello, ma'am," Emily greeted her. "My name's Emily and this is my friend, Mercy."

Mercy nodded her head at the woman, but didn't utter a sound. She kept her eyes averted toward the ground.

"Well, hello Emily and Mercy. What are you doing out in the woods? Where's your parents?"

"Well ma'am. We're traveling back home and uh...well, we...uh," Emily stammered. She didn't know exactly what to tell the woman. She felt Mercy dig her elbow into her ribs.

"Don go tellin' her nuffin 'bout us," Mercy whispered.

The woman looked from Emily to Mercy and then back to Emily. "Tell you what," she said. "Why don't you two come in and let me fix you something to eat, then we can worry about where you're heading."

She stood up out of her rocker and opened the door to the tiny cabin. She realized the girls hadn't budged from their spot in the yard, so she held the door open wide and motioned with her arm for them to come in.

"It's alright. I don't bite," she said.

Emily was the first one to move. She started to take a step forward when Mercy grabbed her arm.

"I don like dis, Em. I's scared."

"Sshhh, it's ok, Mercy. She seems nice."

Emily grabbed Mercy by the hand and drug her up onto the porch and through the open door into the cabin.

The woman indicated two chairs that sat around a small table which was positioned in the middle of the tiny room. Emily pulled out one and sat down. Mercy stood behind her, ready to run at the first sign of danger.

"Mercy, is it?" the woman said to Mercy. "Please have a seat. You're in no danger here."

Mercy, still hesitant, pulled out the other chair and plunked herself down in it.

Dipping a ladle into a bucket she had sitting on the floor next to the table, the woman poured water into three wooden mugs she had taken down from a shelf about the fireplace.

"My name's Mary," she said as she pushed a mug in front of each girl.

Emily guessed that Mary was around Olive's age, which meant she was probably around fifty years old. Her hair, which she wore in a bun, was starting to turn gray around the temples and fine lines were beginning to show around her hazel eyes.

Though she was tall and thin, she had a toughness about her. Emily assumed living out here in the middle of nowhere, a woman had to be strong to survive.

They all jumped at a scratching sound at the door.

Looking around to see what the noise was, they saw that the dog had come up onto the porch and was clawing at the door to get in.

Mary got up and opened the door for him, letting him into the kitchen.

Emily and Mercy just stared with their mouths open as the dog pranced over and sat down at the end of the table.

"I'm guessing this ole boy is yours?" Mary asked, scratching the dog behind his ear.

"No ma'am," Emily said. "He's just been following us for the past two days."

"Well now, if a dog decides to follow you, then he figures you belong to him. So it looks like you've got yourselves a dog."

"He's a mean un. He growled at us yes'day when we comed across 'im," Mercy said, barely above a whisper.

"You're gonna have to speak up a bit if you want me to hear you, young lady. My hearing ain't what it used to be," Mary said. She smiled kindly at Mercy.

"Yes'm," Mercy said. Emily could tell she was still scared and was having a hard time sitting still.

She pulled Mercy's hand into her lap and held it tightly trying to comfort her.

"Now, you say this dog growled at you upon first running into him? Well, I'm guessing he was probably just as surprised to see you as you were to see him. I don't think he has a mean bone in his body. In fact, I think he just needs some TLC."

"What's TLC?" Emily asked.

"Tender loving care," Mary answered.

"The way I see it, this pup just needs some water, some food and plenty of kindness. What are you going to name him?"

Emily looked at Mercy and both girls shrugged.

"Well, he's got to have a name. You can't just go around calling him Dog, now can you?"

"Well, he's not a very pretty dog is he?" Emily asked.

"Not very pretty? He's just downright ugly if you ask me, but he still needs a name."

They all looked at the dog. He was about fifty pounds with short, wiry hair that was a mixture of gray, brown and black. His long legs gave him a gangly appearance. He had a long snout with floppy ears.

"Yeah, he's ugly fo sho," Mercy said.

"Well then, Ugly it is!" exclaimed Mary.

"We're going to call him Ugly?" Emily asked.

"Well, it fits don't it?" Mary said. She gave Ugly a pat on his head and a quick scratch under his chin.

Emily and Mercy giggled as Ugly started thumping his back leg on the floor as Mary scratched him.

"I think he likes it," Emily said.

They all laughed as Ugly wagged his tail, shaking his whole butt.

Mary fixed them all, including Ugly, a quick bite to eat. She'd had stew in a kettle over the fire in the fireplace from an earlier meal, so she warmed it up and served it to her guests.

After they were done eating, Mary cleared away the dishes and sat down at the table again.

"So, tell me how you girls ended up out in the woods. And where did you get those dresses. I know they're not yours."

Mercy pinched Emily's arm, but she just shoved her hand away.

"We were kidnapped from our homes by some men who were going to take us to South Carolina and sell us as slaves."

"I see," Mary said. "Go on."

"We escaped during the night and ran away. We found these dresses on a clothesline at the farm where Ugly found us."

"Uh huh," said Mary. "So you're on the run from some very bad men and you're trying to get home? Where's home?"

"I'm from Pennsylvania. Mercy is from Ohio."

"I see. Do you know where you are right now?" Mary asked.

"No ma'am. I figure we're somewhere in North Carolina?"

"You, my dears, are in South Carolina."

Mercy jumped in her seat. Emily calmly laid her hand on Mercy's arm.

"South Carolina, ma'am?" Emily asked, a tremor in her softly spoken words.

"Yes, dear, South Carolina. Seems you girls ran in the wrong direction."

Emily suddenly felt weak in the knees and her stomach did a flip flop.

"Oh no! We came right to the place where those men were going to bring us!"

"Shush now. It's ok. We're going to figure out just how to get you home," Mary said.

"But how? How are we going to be able to get all the way home from here?" Emily asked.

Mercy sat motionless, not uttering a sound and not moving a muscle. Emily could feel her stiffen up next to her. She knew Mercy was terrified. She was back in the State where her family were former slaves.

"First things first," Mary began. "We need to get you into some clothes that fit you. You'll need good fitting clothes if you're going to be traveling. Hold on one moment. I'll be right back."

Mary got up from the table and scurried into a small room just off the kitchen.

They could hear her in there digging around in something and mumbling to herself.

Soon, she reappeared carrying a stack of clothes in her arms and two pair of boots on top.

Laying them down on the table she said, "Now I know these are young men's clothes, but like I said, if you're going to be traveling, you'll need some good clothes. These used to belong to my son, William. He outgrew them years ago, so I just packed them away in the chest. I figure they'll be of better use letting you have them, then just letting them sit in that old chest and rot."

Emily grabbed up the clothes and examined them. There were two pair of blue wool pants, two white muslin shirts, two black caps and two pairs of black stockings. She separated them, giving Mercy a set.

"I've never worn boy's clothes before, but these sure will be better than this old dress," Emily said.

"I's never wore pants afore," said Mercy, sounding a little giddy.

"Well, go on in the room and change. Let's see how they fit you," Mary said.

Both girls jumped up and ran into the small bedroom. They hastily changed clothes and stepped back out into the kitchen.

They looked each other up and down and giggled. The clothes fit them well and didn't need any adjustments.

"These are quite comfortable, actually," Emily said, spinning around on the spot.

"Deys much better den dem ole dresses," Mercy said.

Mary looked them over appreciatively, nodding her head. "Yes, that's much better. Now try on the boots and see how they fit."

Emily grabbed a pair and slipped her feet into them. They were a tad too big, but she was just glad to have boots again. All the walking through the woods in her bare feet left her with calluses and blisters.

Mercy just shook her head and sat down.

"What, you don't like boots?" Mary asked her.

"I don know iffn I'd like dem or not, ma'am. I's never had any afore."

"Well, try them on. You might like them."

Mercy just shook her head again.

"Well, suit yourself, but they're yours if you want them."

"She wore shoes before and said they hurt her feet. She likes going barefoot better, that's all," Emily told Mary.

"Well, I understand. I prefer going barefoot myself most of the time," Mary said, winking at Mercy.

Mercy gave Mary a big smile. Emily thought Mercy had the most beautiful smile she had ever seen. She could tell she was starting to relax a bit. The worry lines on her forehead had disappeared and her shoulders had relaxed. She liked seeing her friend happy.

"We'll need to do something with that hair of yours, Emily," Mary said. She was scrutinizing Emily's long curls. She began tapping her lip with her finger and scrunching up her eyebrows.

"I got it. We can cut most of it off and you can tuck the rest of it up under the cap," Mary suggested.

Emily looked at her in horror. "What? No, no, no. You can't cut off my hair, please!"

"Oh, oh...ok," Mary stammered. "Ok, so we don't cut off your hair. How about if we braid it then? It'll be a lot less hassle if you at least braid it."

Emily visibly relaxed. Olive used to braid her hair at night to keep it from getting tangled.

"Yes, yes...we can braid it," Emily said.

Mary grabbed some yarn from the sewing basket she had been knitting out of when the girls had arrived. Cutting off a small length of it, she began braiding Emily's hair. Mercy watched the braiding process with fascination.

Once the braid was complete, Mary tied the yarn tightly around the end of it.

"There you go," she said.

"Thank you so much, ma'am."

Mercy reached up and touched her hair. It was short, but curls sprang up in all directions.

"Ya suppose ya could do sumpin wif my hair too?" she asked Mary.

Mary looked curiously at Mercy's hair. "I've never worked with a black girls hair before, but let's see what we can do."

After several failed attempts to do something with Mercy's hair, Mary let out a deep sigh. "I'm sorry, Mercy, I just don't know what to do with it."

"Why don't we just twist little bits of it into braids. Instead of one braid, she can have several," Emily suggested.

An hour later, Emily and Mary stood back to examine their handiwork. Mercy had several tiny braids sticking out all over her head.

"Oh Mercy, you look darling!" Emily exclaimed.

"It does look really cute, if I say so myself," said Mary.

Mercy reached up and felt her head all over. She suddenly burst out laughing.

"It's pufect. I loves it!"

They were all standing there laughing when they heard the sounds of horse's hooves pounding the ground. The sounds were getting closer and closer.

Mary walked over to the door to see who was approaching. A look of fear crossed her face as she turned to the girls.

"Hide!" she whispered hoarsely to them. "Quick now. Hide under the bed in the bedroom. NOW!"

Emily and Mercy dove under the bed and scrunched themselves up as tight as they could. Mercy was shaking and tears where running down her cheeks.

Emily looked out from under the bed and saw their ripped up dresses still laying on the floor near the door. She quickly scrambled out from under the bed and grabbed the dresses. She had just crawled back under when the door to the cabin slammed open. Mercy grabbed her arm and squeezed so hard, Emily thought she would scream in pain, but she pressed her lips firmly together and pulled Mercy closer to her as she recognized the voice of the man who had just entered the cabin.

"We're looking for a couple of runaways, ma'am," said one of the men hired by Mr. Guthrie.

"Do I look like I'm hiding anyone here? Get out of my house," Mary demanded.

"We know they came in this direction. You sure you ain't seen them?"

"I haven't seen anyone come through this way in months."

About that time, Ugly let out a menacing growl. Emily could see him standing next to Mary. His hackles were up and his head was bent low.

"Is that your dog, ma'am?"

"Yes he is."

"Well, you best keep him under control or I'll put a bullet between his eyes," the man growled.

Emily saw Mary lay her hand on Ugly's neck. The dog quieted down a bit, but still stood rigidly beside her.

"We're gonna search your place, so stand aside," said a second man Emily couldn't see.

"Go ahead," said Mary. "But where would I hide anyone in here? There's only this room and a bedroom and it ain't proper for you to go snooping around a widow's bedroom."

The first man looked at the second one and shrugged.

"Well...we need to search...everywhere. These runaways are dangerous and we don't want you getting hurt," said the first man.

"What kind of runaways are you talking about?" Mary asked.

"Well ma'am, they're two young girls, but they are bad, very mean, girls, you see and we're just trying to protect you."

"You're trying to protect me from two *girls*?"

"Well, yes ma'am, but they're mean. They might try to hurt you."

"Get out! Get out now!" Mary stormed. "What kind of idiot do you take me for? Do you think I can't handle two young *dangerous* girls if they came this way? Do I need two strong men to defend me against two girls? Why I could whoop either one of you all by myself. GET OUT!"

Mary shoved the first man out the door. The second man shimmied around her and ran out the door behind the first man.

"Ma'am, we're gonna search your property," called the first man. "We'll be back to search the house in a minute and you'd better let us do it!"

"Or what? You gonna shot me too? You big oafs best get off my property or I'll pump a load of lead into you!" She reached behind the door and pulled out a rifle, cocking the handle she aimed it at them. "Get out of here, I tell you!"

The men high stepped it off of her porch and mounted their horses. Turning around quickly they rode off into the woods.

Mary stood on her porch for a long time making sure the men didn't come back.

Meanwhile, Emily and Mercy stayed hidden under the bed, too afraid to come out.

Eventually, as the sun was setting, Mary came back inside, shutting the door behind her.

"Come on out girls. They're gone now."

Emily crawled out from under the bed, but Mercy wouldn't budge.

"Come on out, Mercy. It's ok. The men are gone," Emily coaxed her.

"Dey'll come back," came Mercy's terrified response.

"No they won't. Mary scared them off."

Mercy slowly emerged from under the bed. The whites of her eyes shone brightly as she jerked her head in every direction listening for the sound of hoof beats.

Mary gently put her arm around Mercy and guided her to the table. "Sit down, Sweetheart. You're safe. I won't let those men come in here."

Mercy accepted the seat, but grabbed Emily's hand and wouldn't let go. Emily gently squeezed her hand and pulled her closer to her side.

"You guys can spend the night here, but tomorrow you'll have to head out. I wish I could let you stay here, but those men will be back and they won't take no for an answer again. I can't afford any trouble. I live here alone now since my husband died and my son went off to fight the war. I hope you understand."

"Yes, ma'am. We understand. We didn't mean to cause you any trouble. We'll leave first thing in the morning," Emily told her.

"I'll make a pallet on the floor and you two can sleep there."

While Mary was preparing a pallet on the floor in the kitchen, Emily and Mercy sat at the table. Neither one said a word as they were both lost in their own thoughts.

When the sun had finally gone down behind the trees and the moon rose high in the sky, the girls curled up on their pallet.

Deep into the night, Emily was still wide awake. She knew neither her nor Mercy would get any sleep that night. They jumped at every little sound and were too afraid to sleep in case the men came back.

Ugly was curled up on the floor next to their pallet, but that didn't stop the girls from being afraid. Emily occasionally reached over and gently laid her hand on him just to make sure he was still there. He would sniff her hand and give it a quick lick, but he never moved away from her.

CHAPTER 8

Morning came all too soon for Emily. She had tossed and turned all night. Now she lay looking up at the ceiling feeling drowsy and irritable.

Mercy rolled over and gently shook her shoulder.

"We gots ta git up and git movin'," she said in a low voice.

"I know."

"Well? What's ya doin' jus layin' dere den?"

Emily sat up and looked down at Mercy.

"I'm scared, Mercy," she said. "We don't know which way to go and those men might still be out there somewhere."

Mercy sat up and reached over Emily to pet Ugly. Ugly thumped his tail on the ground, but didn't move.

"I know. I's scared too."

Mary came out of the bedroom and walked over to the stove. She poured some water into a kettle and placed it over the fire. The fire had been left burning all night, so she stoked the embers until a small flame came to life.

"Good morning, girls," she said as she set mugs on the table. She grabbed a loaf of bread and began cutting off slices and laying them on a plate. When the water began to boil, she filled each mug with the steaming liquid and placed some dry tea leaves in each cup.

"You'll need something in your bellies before you take off today. Eat up."

Emily pulled up a chair and sat down at the table and grabbed a slice of the dry bread. There was a slab of butter on a small plate next to it, so she quickly slathered some butter on the bread, then prepared a slice for Mercy.

Mercy stood behind Emily, but had not yet taken her seat. Emily laid the buttered slice of bread down in front of Mercy's seat and waited for her to sit down.

Mary noticed Mercy and nodded toward the chair. "Best eat up, Mercy. You'll feel better with a full stomach."

"Ma'am," Mercy began. "We's scared. We has no idea where ta go. Can we stay here fer a few more days?"

Mary looked at the girls and a sadness came over her face. She looked down at her feet and slowly shook her head.

"I'm so sorry, but no. I have very little food to feed myself, let alone fill two extra bellies. Union soldiers came through about a month ago and stole most of my hogs and chickens. What I have left will barely last me through this upcoming winter."

Mercy slowly nodded and sat down. She grabbed the bread slice and took a bite. Chewing slowly, tears began to well up in her eyes. A tear slid down her cheek and onto the bread.

"Oh now, come on," Mary said. "If I could keep you I would, but you want to go home right? I couldn't keep you here if you want to go home, now could I?"

Mercy and Emily both shook their heads. Emily reached over and squeezed Mercy's hand. Mercy clung to it and didn't let go.

"It's just….well we don't even know which way to go," Emily said. "When we escaped those men, we just took off without knowing which way we were going. We just wanted to get away from them, but now, we have no idea how to get back home."

Mary pursed her lips and tapped the side of her head as if thinking about something.

"Wait here a moment. I may have something that could help you."

She disappeared into her bedroom. They could hear her digging around in the chest again. Soon she reappeared holding something in her hand.

"Here," she said, handing the object to Emily.

Emily took it and just stared at it for a moment. "What is it?"

"It's a compass," Mary said.

"What does it do?" Emily asked, turning the object over in her hand. It was a small, round, metal object with an arrow inside that rotated around when Emily moved her hand.

"It points North," Mary said. "As long as the arrow is pointing to the N, then you are heading in the right direction."

Mercy grabbed the compass and turned it around in her hand watching the arrow spin around.

"How does it know which way is North?"

"I don't know how it works, but it *does* work. It used to belong to my husband. When he would be out traveling, he would always use it to find his way back home. You see, he wasn't real good with directions."

Mercy walked over to the door and held the compass out in front of her. "It's pointin' dat way," she said, pointing in the direction of the tiny garden.

"Then that's the way you need to go," Mary said. "Just keep following that arrow and it will take you home."

Emily walked over and took the compass from Mercy. She walked around in a circle and watched the arrow spin around in it's little case.

"Wow, that is something else."

Mary swung around quickly and began rummaging around the kitchen. Soon, she pulled a small bag out of a cabinet in the corner. The bag was a mish mash of different material all sewn together. It had a rope strap to carry it over the shoulder. She grabbed a small towel and wrapped the remaining bread in it and dropped it down into the bag. She then, pulled down some cheese from a shelf next to the cabinet and dropped it into the bag as well.

"I know it isn't much, but it should hold you over for a day or two," she said, handing the bag to Emily. "I wish I could do more, but that's all I can afford to part with."

Emily gratefully took the bag and flung it over her shoulder. She rushed over to Mary and threw her arms around her.

"Thank you so much for everything you've done. We'll never forget you."

Mercy gingerly walked over to Mary and held out her hand. "Yes'm," she said. "We tanks ya a lot."

Mary grabbed Mercy by the shoulders and pulled her into a hug.

"You girls are two of the bravest people I've ever met. I pray you have safe travels and may God watch over you as you go."

Emily and Mercy stepped out onto the porch. The sun was shining brightly and the sky was a cloudless, azure blue. Humidity hung heavy in the air and their clothes immediately began sticking to their skin. They stuffed the caps down on their heads and tucked in their shirts.

"Thank you for everything," Emily said again.

"God speed, girls," Mary said. She took a step back to allow the girls to pass.

Emily held the compass out in front of her and saw that the arrow pointed toward the tiny garden off to the side of the house. She stepped down from the porch and headed in that direction with Mercy right behind her.

Ugly, sensing he was about to be left behind, suddenly jumped up from his spot on the floor next to the pallet and rushed out to join them.

Emily kept the compass held tightly in her hand. She had never seen such an instrument before, but she knew it was important to their journey. Without it, they might possibly never make it home. It fascinated her how the arrow spun in different directions depending on which way she pointed it.

The three of them headed off into the woods. Emily leading the way with the compass, followed closely by Mercy. Ugly trotted along at his own pace, but never let too much distance come between them.

As the day wore on, it steadily got hotter. They had not thought to ask Mary for water canteens and now they were soaking wet with sweat and their throats and lips were parched. Ugly's tongue was lolling out of the side of his mouth as he panted with each step he took.

"Mercy, we need to find water," Emily said, smacking her lips together.

"I know. My mouf is so dry it hurts ta swaller."

They walked on for several more minutes when somewhere up ahead they heard water running. Ugly's ears perked up as if he heard it too.

"I think it's a river," Emily said, excitedly. She tucked the compass into the cloth bag for safe keeping and threw it over her shoulder. Picking up her pace, she began jumping over fallen logs and weaving around stumps and overgrowth.

"Wait fer me, Em," Mercy called.

Emily couldn't stop. She was so dry and parched that all she could think about was the cool, clear water of the river. She sped along, heedless of the bushes and thorns that snagged her clothes as she passed by them. Ugly pounced along behind them, seemingly as eager to reach the water as they were.

The sound of the water was getting louder. Emily knew they must be getting close when all of a sudden Mercy lunged at her, jumping on her back and knocking her to the ground. She landed on her hands and knees with Mercy on top of her. Ugly stopped several feet back and began to whimper. He started pawing the ground and running in circles.

"What did you do that for?" Emily demanded.

Mercy clapped her hand over Emily's mouth and pointed.

Across the river, just visible through the trees, were two men. Emily could see it was the men who had been at Mary's the night before. She quickly flattened herself to the ground so they wouldn't see her. Mercy dropped down next to her. Neither one said a word as they watched them. Ugly stayed back where he was, but began growling softly, deep in his throat.

"Sshhh, Ugly," Emily scolded him, turning to see where he was. He stopped growling and cocked his head to one side. He then dropped to the ground and crawled his way a little closer to the girls. Emily just shook her head and turned back to look at the men again.

"I knowed dey'd still be 'round somewhere," Mercy said.

"What are we going to do now?"

"We waits till dey leave."

"What if they don't leave? Or, what if they come this way?" Fear edged Emily's voice as she spoke.

"Hush! Dey gonna hear ya."

They watched the men sitting on the bank of the river. They didn't seem to be in any hurry to leave. Their horses were tied to some trees up the bank from where the men sat. Where did they get the horses from, Emily wondered. They didn't have them when they were with Mr. Guthrie. They must have borrowed, or stolen them, from someone when they started hunting for her and Mercy.

Mercy tapped Emily on the shoulder, jolting her out of her thoughts. When Emily looked at her, Mercy motioned for her to follow her.

"Where are you going?" Emily whispered.

"Sshhh, just come on. I tink we might be able ta go 'round dem."

Mercy crawled on her hands and knees back the way they had come a short distance, then turned to the right and began to follow the river downstream. Emily followed close behind. Ugly watched them curiously for a moment, then ran after them.

Emily was awfully glad she had on pants. The rocky, rough ground would have torn up her knees if she'd still been in a dress. As it was, the rocks poked into her knees and several times she had to stop and rub one of them.

Once they had reached a distance that they could no longer see or hear the men, they made their way back toward the riverbank.

When they got to the bank, they could see that a bend in the river kept them from being seen by the men.

Mercy leaned down and thrust her face into the cool, clear river. Sucking in deep gulps of water, she stopped only to take a breath now and then.

Emily waited till Mercy was done, then she too, got her fill of water. She didn't want to drink at the same time as Mercy, because one of them had to keep a look out for the men.

Ugly stayed back a few feet, but once the girls moved away from the water, he darted forward and lapped up the water too. When he was done, he retreated farther back up onto the bank and sat down to watch over the girls.

With their bellies full of water, the girls laid back on the bank and rested.

Emily was watching the sky. Big, fluffy, white clouds were forming. She lay there trying to find different shapes and figures in the constantly changing clouds.

Mercy suddenly began tapping her arm urgently. Emily thought it might be the men, so she sat up quickly, looking all around.

"What? What it is? Is it the men?" she asked, nervously.

"Nah, look," Mercy said, pointing downriver from where they were. "It's a boat."

Emily scanned the riverbank, but couldn't see what Mercy was seeing.

"Where? I don't see it."

"It's jus dere, behine dem trees."

Mercy quickly got to her feet and began making her way down the river following the bank. Ugly sprang up from his resting place and trotted along after her. Emily still didn't see the boat, but she followed along behind Mercy and Ugly.

As they neared a small stand of trees, Emily saw the end of a boat peeking out from behind some branches.

When they reached it, they realized it must have been there for a long time. Vines were growing over it and it was filled with a bunch of dead leaves and small broken branches.

"Do you think it will still float?" Emily asked. She began tugging on the vines.

"I's hopin' so. Udderwise, we won be able ta git ta far wifout dem men findin' us."

They cleared away the vines and then began digging out handfuls of the leaves and tossing them out of the boat. Ugly jumped and snapped at the leaves as they fell to the ground.

The little rowboat was just big enough for two people to fit in it. A small wooden seat was situated at each end. The faded green wood on the outside was a little warped and peeling, but otherwise, the boat looked in good condition.

When they had most of the debris cleaned out, they pulled the boat down the bank toward the water.

They walked around it looking for holes, but didn't discover any. Mercy leaned down to look inside.

"Look!" She said, excitedly. "Dere's da oars! Dey's tucked up inside!"

They each reached in and pulled out an oar from under the side of the boat they were on. The one Emily pulled out was broken in half, while the one Mercy pulled out was still in one piece.

"Well, we's got one good un, so dat's good," Mercy said, holding the good one up for Emily to see.

They tossed the oars into the boat and grabbed each other's hands and began jumping up and down and squealing. Ugly let out a yip at them as he danced around their feet.

Their celebration was short lived when they heard someone shouting.

"Hey, there they are!" came a man's voice from across the river.

Emily and Mercy stopped jumping and jerked around just in time to see the two men on the opposite bank of the river, one of them pointing over at them. Ugly growled, the hair on his back standing on end.

"Quick, let's get the boat into the river!" Emily said in a panic.

Mercy stood there frozen, just staring at the men.

Emily jerked her arm and shouted at her. "Come on, Mercy! We have to go!"

Emily grabbed one side of the boat, while Mercy grabbed the other. They heaved it down to the water's edge and pushed it in. Ugly came running down the bank and leaped into the boat. He landed squarely in the middle and sat down. Emily looked at Mercy stunned, but threw the bag into the boat and climbed in over him, grabbing the good oar. Taking a seat, she waited for Mercy to climb in.

"They're getting away!" shouted one of the men.

Both men jumped into the water, leaving their horses on the bank, and began swimming toward the girls.

"Hurry, Mercy! Get in!" Emily screeched.

Mercy swung her leg over the side and dragged herself up, but couldn't get her balance and fell into the boat, landing next to Ugly. Emily didn't wait for her to straighten herself out. She stuck the paddle into the water and began paddling as hard as she could. The boat rocked back and forth, but made little surges forward as the paddle pushed through the water.

Emily watched the men swimming toward them. They were getting closer and closer. Soon, one of them was within reach.

Mercy finally gained her seat and turned around to watch, terrified, as the man reached out his hand to grab the side of the boat. Ugly barked and snapped at him, baring his teeth.

Emily stood and raised the paddle she was holding up in the air and brought it down on top of the man's head. He let out a yelp and sank beneath the water. The other man, seeing what happened, began swimming even harder toward them.

Mercy grabbed up the broken oar and dipped it into the water. She began paddling as hard as she could. With both girls paddling, the little boat picked up speed. Soon, the men were left behind, bobbing up and down in the water.

Emily could see blood on the one man's face from where she had whacked him with the oar, but she didn't feel any sympathy for him. She stuck her tongue out at him as she continued to paddle with all her might.

Mercy looked back at the men and stuck her tongue out too. She turned back to Emily and started laughing.

"I's never had da nerve ta do dat afore. It felt good."

They watched the men as they swam back to the shore. As they dragged themselves up onto the bank, they turned to stare after the girls.

Emily watched them for a moment, then looked at Mercy with a worried expression on her face.

"Wha's wrong, Em?" Mercy asked her.

"They'll just ride their horses down river and catch up to us."

Mercy swung around in her seat just in time too see the men grab the horses by the reins, then quickly disappear into the trees.

"Oh no, wha's we gonna do now den?"

Emily just shook her head. They floated in silence for awhile, both deep in thought. The river was calm, but had a strong current which swept the girls farther and farther downstream.

"We needs ta tink of sumfin quick, afore dey catches up wif us," Mercy said.

Emily thought for a moment, then suddenly dipped her oar into the water and started paddling. All she managed to do was turn them in a circle though.

"What're ya doin'?" Mercy asked, confused.

"They think we're going to float on down the river, right? So, that's exactly what we're *not* going to do."

Realizing what she was trying to do, Mercy helped Emily guide the boat to the bank. Once they reached it, they both jumped out and pulled the boat up out of the water. Ugly leaped out onto the bank and ran around sniffing everywhere. After he was satisfied that everything was ok, he laid down and watched the girls tug the boat up into the trees.

"We need to hide the boat so they don't find it," Emily said.

They pulled the boat into the woods a little farther and dropped it next to a tree. They ran around gathering up branches and leaves to cover it with.

Once they had covered it enough that it couldn't be seen from the river, they made their way deeper into the woods.

They knew it wouldn't be long before the men caught up to them. From their hiding spot back in the trees, they could just make out the riverbank on the other side. When the men passed by, they would see them.

Mercy flopped down on the ground behind a fallen log and peered over the top. Emily, next to her, did the same. Ugly assumed his usual position of laying a few feet behind them. He laid his head on his front paws and dozed, seemingly unaware of the danger.

It wasn't long before they caught sight of the men. They were picking their way along the riverbank on their horses. They didn't notice the drag marks up the side of the bank on the other side of the river where the girls had pulled the boat up. They just continued their way down stream and soon, disappeared from sight.

Mercy let out the breath she was holding and rolled over onto her back. Emily continued to watch the river to make sure the men didn't turn around and come back.

CHAPTER 9

The girls stayed hidden behind the log for well over an hour watching the riverbank on the opposite side.

When they were sure that the men had moved on and would not come back, they got up and dusted the dirt and leaves off their clothes.

Mercy looked at Emily and chuckled.

"What's so funny?" Emily asked her.

"Iffn ya was ta put yer hair up inta dat hat, ya'd look jus like a boy," Mercy said.

Emily giggled and tucked her braid up under the cap. "Well? Do I?"

"Yup, ya sho does."

"Tuck yours in too," Emily said.

Mercy tucked her spiky braids up under her hat too and laughed. "Well? Does I look like a boy too?"

Emily was giggling so hard she couldn't talk. Finally, she nodded her head. "Hey, we should keep our hair up like this. If they're looking for girls, they won't look twice at us."

"But dem men already dun saw us in dese boy clothes."

"I know, but maybe they weren't really paying attention."

"Les hope not."

Emily dug around in the bag and pulled out the compass. She swung it around in front of her until the arrow landed on the N.

"This way," she said pointing off into the trees.

"Wait," Mercy said. "Les eat sum of dat bread and cheese Mary packed in dere fo us."

"Good idea," Emily said. She rooted around in the bag and pulled out the bread and cheese and unwrapped it. They sat on the log and began pulling off chunks of bread and stuffing it into their mouths. Ugly's ears perked up and he came over and sat down in front of them.

"We's got ta feed 'im too," Mercy said, looking at Ugly.

Emily tossed him a chunk of bread. He woofed it up and waited for her to throw him some more.

"We can't give it all to him or we won't have any," Emily complained.

"We's lucky ta have any a'tall. So we need ta share it wif 'im."

Emily had the grace to look ashamed. She tossed Ugly another chunk of bread.

When they finished their meager lunch, they stuffed the remaining bread and cheese back into the bag and set off in the direction the arrow indicated.

They walked through the woods for hours. The humidity only got worse as the day wore on and the heat rising from the floor of the forest was almost suffocating. The rotting smell of old wood and damp earth filled their nostrils as they trudged along.

By now it was getting close to evening. The sun was low in the sky and crickets had already started their serenading.

Emily was dragging her feet and her shoulders were slumped over. "How do you keep on going?" she asked Mercy.

Mercy was a good ten feet in front of her and was still keeping up a good pace. "I's used ta da heat."

"How? I can't take another step," Emily whined.

"I werked in da heat all day long. We weren't allowed ta stop till da sun went down."

"Seriously? How horrible!" Emily exclaimed.

"Dat's jus da way it is fo us blackies."

"I don't care. That isn't right."

"Wha we s'posed ta do 'bout it? Iffn we stopped, we didn't git paid."

Ugly was plodding along behind them, when he suddenly let out a sharp bark and bounded ahead.

"What's up with him?" Emily asked.

"I don know," Mercy said, looking to see where he went.

They could see the trees thinning out and Ugly sitting at the edge of the tree line.

"We's comin' up ta sumpin," Mercy said softly.

"Another farm?"

"I don tink so. I tink it's a town," Mercy said.

Emily peered around Mercy to see buildings off in the distance through the trees.

"Should we go through the town or try to go around it?"

"We needs ta find a place ta sleep fo da night. Mebbe we could find us a place in da town. It sho would beat sleepin' in da woods again."

"Looks like Ugly agrees," Emily said. Ugly had jumped up and trotted through the remaining trees and out onto a dusty road.

They followed the road into a small, but busy town. There was only one street that ran the length of it. The road they came in on trailed off into the woods, while the other end took off through fenced in fields that were full of cows and sheep and a few horses. There was a bank, a tavern, a livery stable, a small mercantile and a sheriff's office. Several other buildings lined the street and at the end was a large two story building surrounded by a tall fence. Emily noticed several young kids playing in the yard, but didn't pay much attention. Maybe it was a schoolhouse or something, she thought.

They made their way down the street trying to look inconspicuous. Whenever someone would walk past them, they would duck their heads and look in the opposite direction. This was hard to do at times because there were a lot of people milling about and horse-drawn wagons zipped up and down the street. If they weren't careful, they could easily get run over.

Ugly seemed to be enjoying himself. He darted in and out of the oncoming wagons and sniffed each person who passed by.

Finally, Emily grabbed Mercy's arm and pulled her down an alley that ran beside the tavern. Ugly seemed completely uninterested in stopping, so he continued his investigation of things and disappeared down the street.

Leaning up against the wall, Emily let out a deep sigh. "I'm hungry and tired."

"Me too," Mercy said. She slumped down to the ground with her back to the wall. Emily copied her.

"Where are we going to stay for the night?" Emily asked, yawning deeply.

"How 'bout da livery stable," Mercy said, pointing to the building at the end of the street.

Emily looked in the direction Mercy was pointing. The livery stable was at the end of the street, set back away from the other buildings. Probably to keep the smell of the horses from the other establishments. It was a weathered, gray, wooden building with a big door in the front. A man was sitting on an old rickety chair beside the door.

"What are we supposed to do, walk up to that man and ask him if we can sleep in there?" Emily asked.

"No silly," Mercy said, shaking her head. "We's gonna sneak in da back door and crawl up inta da hayloft."

"Won't that man hear us? He's sitting right there!"

"He gonna be drunker dan a skunk afore long."

"How do you know that?" Emily asked.

"Look at 'is feet. He gots a bottle of sumpin sittin' dere. I's bettin' it's whiskey or sumpin like dat."

Emily squinted her eyes and sure enough, there was a bottle sitting on the ground next to the man. "How do you know that's whiskey?"

"I's seen enuf ta know. Jus trust me."

Emily was getting ready to say something when a woman came out of the back door of the tavern and spotted them sitting there. She was dressed in a big, flouncy gown the color of a tangerine. Her breasts were pushed up so far, they almost fell out of the top of her dress. Her blond hair was piled on top of her head so high, Emily wondered how she didn't topple over. Her face was painted heavily with rouge and lipstick. It was so heavy that she almost looked like a clown that Emily had seen once when her father had taken her to see the circus. The woman clapped her hands over her mouth and made a soft squealing noise. She rushed over to them and leaned down, scrutinizing every inch of them. A strong, pungent smell wafted through the air around her. It smells of sweet flowers and cigar smoke.

"Oh, you poor little boys," she said. "What are you doing out here all alone? Where are you folks?"

Emily just stared at the woman with her mouth open. Mercy gaped at her as well. Neither girl knew what to say.

Finally, after waiting for an answer, but getting none, the woman winked and said, "I know what's going on here. You guys are runaways aren't you?"

Emily started to get up to run, but the woman gently laid her hand on her shoulder. "It's ok. I won't tell anyone. I've been there myself before. But I bet you must be hungry."

Emily and Mercy both slowly nodded their heads. They were both very leery of the woman and were not sure what to make of her.

"You boys stay right here. I'll go inside and see if I can rustle you up some grub. I'll be right back." She disappeared back into the tavern leaving Emily and Mercy sitting there staring after her.

"She thinks we're boys," Emily finally said. She looked at Mercy with a shocked look on her face. Mercy burst out laughing. Emily realized that that is what they wanted people to think and so, she too, started laughing.

Ugly chose that moment to come prancing down the alley toward them. He seemed wore out. His tongue was hanging out the side of his mouth and he was panting hard. He flopped down next to Mercy and laid his head in her lap.

The sun was just about ready to drop out of sight and the temperatures were finally beginning to cool down a little. Emily glanced down the street toward the livery stable and saw the man guzzling down whatever was in that bottle. He swayed on his seat for a moment, then stood up and vanished into the shadows of the stable. Emily hoped he was going to go pass out somewhere. Maybe they would be able to sneak up to the hayloft after all. He certainly staggered off like he was drunk.

The woman returned a few moments later carrying two plates. She stopped when she saw Ugly. "Oh no! I didn't know you had a dog. I'll have to go back in and grab some scraps for him."

She carried the plates over to them and handed one to each girl. Each plate contained a piece of chicken, mashed potatoes and cornbread. The smell of the food made Emily's stomach lurch and growl. She quickly took the plate and laid it on her lap. Mercy took her plate and immediately began digging into the hot meal.

"Thank you, ma'am," Emily said. "We really appreciate this."

"Yes,m, tank ya," Mercy said around a mouthful of food.

The woman nodded at them and watched them eat a few bites, then seemed to remember Ugly.

"I'll go see about some scraps for him," she said.

Again, she disappeared into the tavern, returning moments later with a bowl full of scraps for Ugly. She set the bowl down in front of him and stepped back. He sniffed the contents, then scarfed it down in a couple of gulps.

When the girls had finished their meals, they handed the plates back to the woman and thanked her again.

"You boys are very welcome," she said. "Where do you plan on spending the night?"

Emily didn't like the way she asked the question. She almost seemed like she was up to something, but before she could answer her, Mercy spoke up. "We's headed outta town ma'am. We's not gonna be stayin' here nowhere."

Emily looked at Mercy, but decided not to question her about it. Instead, she looked up at the woman and just nodded.

"Well, ok then," the woman said, eyeing them suspiciously.

Mercy quickly got to her feet and grabbed Emily by the hand and hauled her up next to her. "Well, we's gonna git goin' now. Tank ya again fo da grub."

With that, Mercy took off toward the main street, dragging Emily along with her. Ugly trotted along behind them, still licking his chops.

They scurried down the street away from the tavern, but in the opposite direction of the stable. Once they were far enough away from the woman and the tavern, Emily pulled on Mercy's hand to stop her. They ducked into a shadowy spot between the bank and the sheriff's office.

"Why did you lie to that woman?" she asked.

"Cause dat woman was up ta sumpin. Did ya see dat look in her eyes?"

"Yeah, I did. I wonder what she was going to do?"

"I don know, but we wasn't gonna stick 'round ta find out."

"I'm glad you spoke up, Mercy. I almost told her the truth."

"I's afeared ya was gonna tell her, so dat's why I tole her dat so fast."

Emily gave Mercy a quick hug and stepped back. Mercy looked at her like she was daft.

"Wha ya do dat fo?"

"Because I'm glad we're friends. I don't know what I would do without you, Mercy Dunn!"

"Mercy Dunn? You callin' me by yer last name?"

"Well, yes, I suppose I am. From now on, you're my sister. We are sisters."

Mercy just shook her head, but she had a huge grin on her face. "Yous jus crazy."

Emily reached out and grabbed Mercy's hand and gave it a big squeeze. "I've always wanted a sister and now I have the best one ever."

"Yup, yous jus crazy."

They stayed in the shadows between the two buildings until the sun had gone down and darkness covered the town. Most of the people had gone indoors or had driven out of town on their wagons and the town was becoming still and quiet.

Mercy stuck her head out from around the side of the building and surveyed the streets. Making sure the coast was clear, she grabbed Emily's hand and they made their way toward the stable, ducking in between buildings and sticking to the shadows whenever someone came along.

Ugly seemed to understand the need to hide and stayed behind them, occasionally popping his head out around a building to look around, but never running ahead.

They finally reached the livery stable and quietly slipped around to the back. The man who had been sitting out front earlier was nowhere to be seen. Emily hoped he was gone for the night, but she kept her eyes open, watching for him with each step they took.

They slipped into the barn by way of a door on the back of the building that was slightly ajar. Mercy squeezed through first, with Emily following right behind her. Ugly seemed to hesitate, but stepped through when Emily coaxed him a little.

The inside of the stable was dark except for a single lantern that was hanging on a nail next to one of the stalls. The smell of sweaty horses and old leather filled the room. A soft snoring sound could be heard coming from one of the stalls toward the front of the building. Mercy and Emily tiptoed up to the stall where the snoring was coming from and glanced inside. The man from outside was laying on a pile of hay sound asleep.

Mercy placed her finger to her lips and backed away slowly. Emily nodded and followed her.

Suddenly Ugly darted out around them and walked into the stall with the snoring man. He proceeded to sniff him all over.

"Ugly..." Emily whispered urgently. "Come on, get out of there."

Ugly continued to sniff the man and then to the girls horror, licked the man's face. The man snorted in his sleep and wiped the back of his hand across his face, but kept on sleeping.

Mercy and Emily quickly backed away from the stall and headed toward the back door, hoping for a quick escape.

Emily grabbed Mercy's arm to stop her. "He didn't wake up," she whispered as close to Mercy's ear as she could get.

They stood in the middle of the barn for several moments, but no stirring or movement could be heard, except for the occasional stomp of the only horse in the barn. Ugly finally came out of the stall and sat down next to Emily and licked his lips.

"You're just stupid, you know that," she scolded him, quietly.

Mercy looked around and found the ladder that led to the loft. She tapped Emily on the shoulder and pointed to it. Emily nodded and pushed Mercy toward it. They silently ascended the ladder and made their way to the back of the loft. Ugly was unable to climb the ladder so he laid down at the bottom of it and crossed his front paws. He laid his head down on his paws and let out a deep sigh. Within minutes, he was sound asleep.

The girls hunkered down in the hay and got comfortable. The straw poked through their clothes and was itchy against any bare skin, but it was still better than sleeping on the ground in the woods.

"What are we going to do tomorrow?" Emily asked Mercy in a hushed whisper.

"We's gonna head outta town and continya ta head Norf."

Emily remembered the compass and pulled the bag off her back and fished around in it till she located the compass. The metal was cool in her hand, but the knowledge of it's purpose warmed her heart. She gave it a quick squeeze and tucked it back into the bag.

Mercy curled up on her side facing Emily. She removed her cap and laid it under her head to keep the straw from jabbing her in the scalp. "I really like boy's clothes."

Emily laid down next to Mercy facing her too. She removed her cap and placed it under her head as well. "Me too. They're so much more comfortable than girl's clothes. I don't ever want to wear a dress again."

"Me neither," Mercy said. "G'night, Em."
"Good night, Mercy."

They snuggled up close to each other and soon were fast asleep.

Neither of them noticed the figure peering at them over the top of the ladder, nor did they hear Ugly's soft growls.

CHAPTER 10

Emily was rudely awakened by something chattering in her ear. Turning her head, she came face to face with a mouse. "Eek!" she shrieked, jumping to her feet. She began mussing up her hair to make sure the mouse had not climbed onto her head.

"Wha's wrong?" Mercy asked, sitting up and looking around.

"A mouse! A mouse was sitting by my head!"

"Well, keep yo voice down. You's gonna wake da whole town."

From somewhere below them on the main floor of the barn, they heard someone rustling around. Emily looked at Mercy, panic etched into her face. "It's the man from the stall," she whispered to Mercy.

"We needs ta git outta here," Mercy said.

Emily grabbed her cap up off the hay and crammed it down on her head. Slinging the bag with the compass in it over her shoulder, she followed Mercy to the ladder.

Mercy stepped onto the ladder and began her descend when she was suddenly grabbed from behind and lifted off the ladder. She was swung around and dropped onto the floor. She landed roughly on her backside. Emily saw the man grab Mercy and drop her. She quickly stepped back away from the ladder.

"Come on now, lad," the man who had been sitting outside the barn the night before, said gruffly. "I know you're up there. Get on down here."

Emily cautiously made her way to the ladder and looked down at the man. He motioned for her to come down. "Come on," he said. "Let's go."

Emily turned around and placed her foot on the first rung. She had barely made it to the second rung when the man's large hands lifted her off the ladder and dropped her to the ground next to Mercy.

"What are you lads doing up there?"

"We's jus sleepin' up dere, sir," Mercy said.

"This ain't no inn. You ain't allowed to be sleeping in here. Now get on out of here before I call the sheriff."

Emily grabbed Mercy's hand and they turned to run out of the barn, but Mercy stopped suddenly bringing Emily up short. Turning back to the man, she asked, "Where's our dawg?"

"What dog?" the man asked.

"Nevermind, let's just go," Emily said urgently, tugging on Mercy's hand.

They ran out of the barn and just as they made it onto the main street, the woman from the tavern stepped out of the sheriff's office with the sheriff right behind her. She saw the girls and grabbed the sheriff by the arm and shouted, "That's them, Sheriff. I told you they were still here somewhere!"

Emily and Mercy turned to run, but the sheriff took off after them. "Stop right there, boys!"

The lady from the tavern put her hand to her throat and watched as the sheriff took off after the girls. Emily and Mercy were no match for a grown man and he quickly caught up to them. Reaching out, he snagged Emily by the scruff of her collar and jerked her backward off her feet. He reached out for Mercy, but missed.

"Run Mercy!" Emily shouted to her.

Mercy glanced back over her shoulder and saw that the sheriff had Emily by the collar. She turned and kept on running. Emily watched her run down the street, then turn and disappear around the side of a building.

"Well, well, well, what do we have here," the sheriff asked Emily. "A runaway?"

"I'm not a runaway, sir," Emily said, trying to explain.

He shook her by her collar and put his face down close to hers. "Then where are your parents? Why are you and that other little boy all by yourselves?" He sneered at her and gave her another shake.

"We're on our way home, sir. We aren't runaways."

"Yeah, right," he said. "I've got the perfect place for you." He began dragging her down the street. The lady from the tavern stood on the side of the street and watched them pass. Emily looked over at her and could have sworn she saw a tear in the lady's eye.

The sheriff hauled her all the way down to the two story building with the fence around it that Emily had seen the day before. He stopped at a gate in front of the building and called out to someone. "Hey Eliza! I got someone for you!"

Emily glanced up at him, but he ignored her and kept his eyes on the front door of the building.

Soon, an older woman with gray hair piled high on her head, opened the door. She was short and plump and had the distinct air of someone in charge. She marched down the steps and over to the gate. Emily saw by the look on her face that she was not happy to have been disturbed. "What have you got there, Sheriff? Another runaway? What am I supposed to do with him? I'm running out of room in here, you know." She puffed up her ample bosom and pursed her lips. She gave Emily a once over and said, "Well, bring him in, then."

Pulling a key from her pocket, she unlocked the gate and pulled it open. The sheriff pushed Emily through, still holding onto her collar. He walked her up to the front door and turned to Eliza. "There was another one, but he got away. If he's smart, he'll keep running, but if I catch him, I'll be bringing him to you too. Oh, and he's a blackie."

The woman shook her head vehemently. "I don't need no blackies in here. I have enough trouble with the white ones. If you find him, just run him off. I'll not be allowing his kind in my fine establishment."

"Whatever you say, Eliza," the sheriff said with a sad shake of his head.

Eliza grabbed Emily by the arm and yanked her to her side. "I've got him from here, Sheriff. You can head back to your office now."

The sheriff tipped his hat to Eliza and turned to leave. He strolled down the sidewalk and out through the gate.

Eliza jerked Emily around to face her. "You wait right here while I go lock up that gate. Move one muscle and it will be no supper for you tonight."

Tears ran down Emily's face as she watched Eliza waddle to the gate and snap the lock into place.

When Eliza returned to Emily, she grabbed her by the arm and shoved her inside the house. "There will be no crying here. You will behave yourself or it will be the woodshed for you. Do you understand?"

Emily merely nodded and wiped her eyes on the back of her sleeve. She pondered whether or not to tell Eliza that she was a girl, but decided against it. It was best to let her believe she was a boy. Maybe that way, they wouldn't force her back into a dress.

The inside of the building was gloomy and drab. The gray painted walls and old wooden floors showed years of usage and neglect. Gas lights along the wall did little to change the dreariness of the place.

Eliza led Emily up a set of stairs to the left of the doorway. The steps were steep and creaky with remnants of old carpet barely covering them.

At the top of the steps, they turned right and walked down a long hallway to a room at the end of the hall. Eliza pulled the keys out of her pocket again and unlocked the door. Swinging the door open, she shoved Emily inside. "This will be your room for now. If you behave, you can stay here. If you can't, then you will be moved to the basement. Do you understand me?"

Emily nodded her head. Eliza reached out and slapped her across the face. "When you are asked a question, I expect you to answer me. Now, I asked you if you understood."

"Yes, ma'am," Emily said, stiffly. She refused to rub her cheek where Eliza had struck her. She didn't want to give Eliza the satisfaction of knowing she had hurt her.

"That's better. Get settled in. Dinner is at six o'clock sharp. One of the other boys will be around to let you out. You will be locked in your room at all times till you learn the rules around here. Do you understand?"

"Yes, ma'am," Emily said.

"Do you have any questions for me?"

"No, ma'am."

"Good. Then I will see you at dinnertime."

Eliza turned on her heel and shut the door behind her. Emily heard the lock slide into place and the sound of Eliza's footsteps disappearing down the hall.

Emily looked around the room. There were two single beds. One on each side of the room. A single, small desk with a broken chair pushed up under it sat against the wall between the two beds. Years of grime and dust coated the only window in the room. A single, tattered, dirty, gray curtain hung limp on a bent rod over the window. The room smelled of musty old clothes and sweat.

Emily sat down on the bed nearest the door and began to cry. What was going to happen now? Where was Mercy? Where had Ugly gone? Why wasn't he there to protect them? Hadn't Mary said that Ugly would protect her and Mercy? She hoped Mercy just kept running. She had heard what Eliza had told the sheriff. She didn't want Mercy in her house. What would happen to Mercy if the sheriff did catch her? Fresh tears streamed down her cheeks.

Eventually, Emily dried her eyes. Grabbing the bag, she pulled it onto her lap. Eliza hadn't taken it from her and hadn't searched it either. Emily reached in and grabbed the compass. Pulling it from the bag, she squeezed it gently in her hand. She didn't want Eliza to find it and take it from her. She placed it back in the bag and slid the bag under the bed. Maybe Eliza hadn't noticed she even had the bag. If not, then she wanted to keep it that way. She stuffed the bag even further under the bed until it was completely out of sight.

At promptly six o'clock, Emily heard a key in the lock. The door swung open and a young man stood in the doorway and looked at her. "Time for dinner," he said.

Emily stood up and walked over to him. "Hi, I'm Em….Emory," she said, quickly catching herself. She had to make them all think she was a boy. She stuck out her hand for the young man to shake.

"Hi, I'm Thomas," he said, shaking her hand.

"What is this place?" Emily asked him as she followed him out into the hallway. He looked to be a couple of years older than her, but he had a kindness about him. Emily immediately knew she would like him.

"It's an orphanage of sorts. Miss Eliza takes in any kid that doesn't have a home, whether they're orphaned or runaways, or whose parents just don't want them."

"How long have you been here?"

"I've been here for about five years now, I guess. My parents were killed in a buggy accident. The horse spooked at something and jumped over the road into the ditch. The buggy overturned on them and killed them. I didn't have any family who wanted me, so I came here."

"That's horrible. I'm so sorry," Emily said.

"It's ok. It's not so bad here as long as you follow the rules."

"What are the rules?"

"We go over them every night at dinner, so you'll find out soon enough. Come on now, we don't want to be late. That's rule number three -never be late for dinner."

They hurried down the hall to the stairs. They quickly descended down to the main floor and down a hallway toward the back of the house.

They came to a large room full of long tables with rows of chairs along each side. All of the chairs were full, except the two she and Thomas were to sit in.

The room was painted a dull yellow and large windows opened up onto a large yard. A cool breeze blew through the open windows and offered a little relief from the stifling heat of the room.

Emily and Thomas took their seats just as Eliza walked into the room. She stood at the head of the table and clapped her hands together.

"Ok children," she chimed out. "Time to recite the rules. Any newcomers pay attention. You will be expected to learn these and obey each one." She looked directly at Emily as she said this.

"Rule number one," everyone in the room said in unison. "Speak only when spoke to. Rule number two-always answer a question with a verbal response. Rule number three-never be late for dinner. Rule number four-keep your room tidy and clean. Rule number five-no fighting."

The rule repeating went on for several more minutes, but Emily's mind began to wander. She looked around the room at all the others kids. There must have been about twenty to twenty five of them. There were boys and girls alike ranging in ages from around three to fifteen. Emily couldn't help but feel sorry for the littlest ones. They had years before they would be able to leave. She just couldn't imagine living here for that long.

Thomas suddenly tugged on her sleeve and she realized that everyone was taking their seats. She had been so lost in her thoughts that she had remained standing. Quickly sliding into her seat next to Thomas, she stole a quick glance up at Eliza. Her eyes were narrowed and her lips were pursed, but she didn't say anything. She just stared at Emily for a moment then took her seat.

"Don't get on her bad side," Thomas whispered close to her ear. "She can get real mean."

"Thanks, but I don't plan to. She slapped me earlier for nodding at her."

"Rule number two," Thomas said, nodding.

"Yeah, I learned that one."

The food was piled high on platters and passed down the table. Each person took a small helping and passed it on. When it reached Emily, she dug the spoon into the potatoes and dropped a large helping onto her plate. Thomas quickly reached over and scooped some of it onto his plate, then passed the platter to the next kid.

"Only take small amounts. If there isn't enough to go around, Miss Eliza will come check each plate and if you have more than anyone else, she'll take your plate from you and you'll be sent to your room without dinner. Rule number eleven."

Emily accepted the next platter from the kid beside her. It was filled with slices of meat. She took only one slice and passed the platter to Thomas. He gave her a quick nod and took one slice himself. So it went for the rest of the platters. There were four in all. Emily realized that even taking smaller helpings, her plate was full. She started to take a bite, but looked around her to see what the other kids were doing first. She realized that they all sat with their hands in their laps, not touching their food yet.

Thomas leaned in to her and said, "Rule number nine-do not eat until everyone has their food."

Once the platters were set in the middle of the table, all the children picked up their forks at the same time and began shoveling the food into their mouths. Emily looked at Thomas, who nodded at her, so she began to eat her food.

The noise of everyone's forks scraping their plates was almost deafening. Emily grabbed up her water glass and took a large gulp. She noticed that when the kids had cleaned their plates, they sat back in their chairs and folded their hands in their laps.

When everyone was done eating, Eliza stood up from her chair and picked up her plate. All at once, every one of the kids stood up, shoved their chairs back and picked up their plates. In unison, they all shoved their chairs under the table and began to walk, single file, out of the room and around the corner. Emily quickly followed suit and discovered that each child carefully placed their plate on a large counter that ran the length of a kitchen was was behind the dining room. Setting her plate on the counter along with the others, she followed them out of the kitchen and into a large common area.

Everyone took a seat on the floor around Eliza, who sat in a chair with a book perched on her knee.

"Story hour," Thomas informed her.

Emily took a seat on the floor next to Thomas and listened to Eliza read a story from the Bible. She had heard this story before. Her father read it to her often. It was the story of Noah and the ark.

When the story hour was over, all the children were sent to their rooms. They filed out of the common room quietly and climbed the stairs to the different bedrooms they were assigned to.

"You're lucky you get a room to yourself," Thomas told her as they climbed the stairs. "Most of us have to share a room. Some have four to a room."

"Why do I get a room all to myself?" Emily asked.

"You're new. She wants to see how you'll do before she assigns you a roommate."

"I don't want a roommate. I rather like having the room to myself."

"You won't have a choice. If you're lucky, she'll assign you a boy who is nice and won't cause you any trouble."

"I'd like to have you as a roommate then."

"I would like that too, but we don't get a say in it. She'll choose who she thinks is best."

Emily hoped she would be given someone who was as nice and kind as Thomas. She was starting to wish now that Eliza knew she was a girl. It was going to be very awkward sharing a room with a boy.

Thomas unlocked her room for her and let her in. "I'm sorry, but I have to lock the door. Rule number twelve-all doors must be locked at night."

"It's ok. I understand. How did you get put in charge of locking the doors?"

"I've been here so long and I have never given Miss Eliza any reason not to trust me."

"Oh," said Emily. "Good night, Thomas."

"Good night, Emory. Sleep well."

It was strange being called Emory, but she knew it was too late to tell them she was a girl. She feared it would get her into a heap of trouble if Eliza found out now. She would just have to make sure she paid attention to what was going on around her so she didn't give away the fact she wasn't a 'he'.

Emily walked over to the window and looked out. It was almost dark now and the stars were just beginning to pop out in the blackening sky. Her bedroom was on the side of the house where the road disappeared into the trees. This house was the last one on the main street. Beyond it, the road wandered off to who knew where. Emily grabbed her bag from under the bed again and pulled out the compass. She held it toward the window. The road actually pointed North. She released a deep sigh and put the compass back in the bag and shoved it under the bed again.

She flopped down on the bed and lay for a long time looking up at the ceiling. The room was sweltering hot, so she got up and pushed the window open. A warm breeze blew into the room, but it didn't offer much relief. She laid back down on the bed and before long, drifted off to sleep.

CHAPTER 11

Sometime later, Emily was awakened by small thuds on the roof and along the side of the house. She sat up in bed just as a small pebble came sailing through the open window and barely missed hitting her in the head.

Scrambling out of bed, she ran to the window. Looking out into the darkness, she could vaguely make out a form standing just on the other side of the fence. She squinted her eyes, but could not make out who or what it was.

A yippy bark could be heard from down below. Emily could just make out a small figure running up and down the fence line.

"Ugly? Is that you?" she asked softly, leaning out the window. An excited whimper was her answer. She saw something else begin to move back and forth along the fence as well. Just as she was about to call out again, a voice cut through the darkness.

"Em? Em, can ya sees me?" Mercy called out from the dark.

"Mercy?"

"Yup, it's me."

"Oh Mercy, I was so scared I'd never see you again!" Emily said. She leaned out the window trying to see her better, but Mercy's skin was so black it was impossible to see her in the darkness. The moon wasn't bright enough to cast any light on her either. The only thing visible was the white muslin shirt she had on.

"I's gonna git ya outta dere."

"How? I'm locked in my room and can't get out!"

"Can ya climb down da winder?"

Emily leaned out over the window sill and looked down. She was on the second story. There was no way she could jump. It was just too far down. There were no trees close to the window either.

"It's too far to jump. I can't get down," she said.

"Don worry. I's gonna figger sumpin out."

Ugly continued to race up and down the fence, occasionally letting out little yips and whines. Emily was afraid he might make enough noise to wake the others in the house, but before she could tell him to be quiet, she heard a key rattle in the lock on her door. She stuck her head out the window and called down to Mercy, "Someone's coming. I'll be right back!"

She turned away from the window and rushed over to her bed, throwing herself on it just as Thomas swung the door open and walked in.

"What's going on in here?" he asked, looking around. "I heard thumps on the house and I thought I heard you talking to someone."

Emily glanced at the window and then back to Thomas. Having seen her look toward the window, he walked over and stuck his head out. "Who's out there?" he called into the darkness. No one answered him.

"What's going on, Emory?"

"Can I trust you, Thomas?" Emily asked him.

"Yes, you can. We're friends, remember?"

Emily threw caution to the wind and blurted out, "My friend Mercy is down there. She's going to try to get me out of here."

"Wait, what? Slow down. Who's out there?"

"I don't have time to explain right now, Thomas. She's waiting for me and I don't want to stay here any longer."

"She? There's a girl down there? How is she going to get you out of here?"

"Look Thomas, I'm really a girl. My name is Emily, not Emory. And I'm not a runaway. I was kidnapped and brought down here. Mercy and I escaped from the kidnappers and got away. Now we're trying to get back home. Will you help me or not?"

Thomas was shaking his head and blinking rapidly. "What? You're a girl?"

"Thomas…," Emily said, shaking his arm gently. "I have to get out of here. Will you help me?"

"Yeah...yes, I guess," he said, still seemingly confused by all of this. "But you can't go out the window. You'll fall to your death."

"There's no other way out but through the window," Emily argued.

Thomas held the keys up in his hand and dangled them in front of her face. "Yes, there is."

Emily threw her arms around him and hugged him tightly for a moment. "Thank you," she said. She rushed back to the window and leaning out, calling down to Mercy, "Mercy, are you still there?"

"I's righ' here, Em."

"Thomas is going to help. Stay there and be quiet!"

"Who's Thomas?" Mercy called back up.

Emily ignored the question and turned back to Thomas. "Ok, I'm ready. Just let me grab my bag." She reached under the bed and pulled out her bag. Flinging it over her shoulder, she headed for the door.

"Wait," Thomas said. "We can't just go stomping out the door and downstairs. Someone will hear us."

"What do we do then?"

"We have to be very quiet. If Miss Eliza hears us, we'll be in deep trouble. We need to get downstairs and head to the kitchen. There's a door that leads out to the yard from there. Now follow me, but be very quiet. We don't want anyone to hear us."

"Ok, I'll be super quiet. I promise."

"Good, now no more talking."

Thomas cautiously stuck his head out into the hallway and listened for a moment. Emily stayed behind him and didn't make a single noise. Her nerves were on edge and she was feeling a little giddy. She was so excited to see Mercy again. She couldn't wait to get outside and run far away from this place.

When Thomas was sure that everyone was still asleep and no one had heard them, he stepped out into the hallway. The floor squeaked under his foot and he froze. No noise came from anywhere in the house, so he continued toward the stairs, tiptoeing as he went. Emily followed closely behind him, listening very carefully for any noises or sounds that indicated someone knew they were out of their rooms.

They crept down the stairs, taking one at a time. The old, worn out carpet on the steps helped to muffle the sound of their feet as they slowly and carefully made their way to the bottom.

Once down, they turned back toward the kitchen and inched their way down the hallway by running their hands along the wall. It was dark in the house. None of the gas lights were left on during the night and no moonlight filtered through any of the windows. Emily blindly reached out and grabbed a handful of Thomas's shirt. She didn't want to trip over anything or knock into something. They were so close to making it outside, she was starting to get butterflies in her stomach. She held her breath as they entered the kitchen.

"Ok, Emory...I mean, Emily," Thomas whispered back to her. "Almost there. Just a few more steps."

They were almost to the door, when Emily stepped out from behind him and right into a chair that she didn't see sitting there in the dark. The chair scooted across the floor making a loud screeching noise. At the same time, Emily tripped over it and went head over heals onto the floor. "Aarrgghh," she cried out loudly.

The sound seemed to echo through the whole house. Jumping to her feet, she and Thomas froze.

From upstairs, they heard footsteps moving around.

Thomas fumbled around with the keys, trying several in the lock, but not finding the right one. "I can't see what I'm doing! It's too dark," he frantically whispered.

"Hurry, Thomas, hurry!" Emily said. "Someone's coming!"

She turned around and looked back in the direction of the stairs. She couldn't see anyone, but the footsteps were getting quicker and louder. They were now at the top of the stairs. The light from a lantern was casting eerie shadows on the wall just outside the kitchen. She knew whoever it was would be there soon.

Suddenly a key slid into the lock and the door swung open. Thomas grabbed Emily by the sleeve of her shirt and yanked her out the door. He quickly slammed the door shut and they raced across the yard to the fence.

On the other side of the fence, Mercy started jumping up and down. "Hurry up guys. Some'un is comin'," she said.

Several windows in the house begin to light up as children peered out the window at them, holding lanterns up to see who was out there.

"How do we get over the gate?" Emily asked in a panic.

"Over here," Mercy said, running a little further down the fence. "Ugly's bin diggin' a hole!"

Thomas and Emily followed Mercy until they came to where they saw Ugly digging frantically under the fence. He had managed to dig a good size hole large enough for them to crawl through.

Suddenly the kitchen door swung open and Eliza rushed out carrying a lantern. Her hair was hanging in a long braid down her back and she was wearing only her nightdress, which was flapping around her ankles as she ran toward them.

"Get under the fence," Thomas yelled, pushing Emily down to the ground. "Hurry!"

Emily dropped to her stomach and began squirming her way under the fence. She got through easily enough and turned to Thomas. "Thomas, come on!" she yelled to him.

He turned just as Eliza was almost upon him. He suddenly dropped to his knees and crawled under the fence to join Emily and Mercy on the other side. He had just pulled his legs through when Eliza reached them.

"THOMAS!" she bellowed. "Get back in here NOW!"

Thomas looked at Emily and Mercy, then back to Eliza. "Not this time, Miss Eliza. I figure I'm old enough now to be on my own. Thanks for everything." He tossed the house keys over the fence to her.

"You get back here now or I'll go get the sheriff," she stormed at him.

"You'd better get going then," Thomas told her. "But by the time he gets here, we'll be long gone."

With that, he, Emily and Mercy took off running down the road. Ugly snorted and shook the dirt off his nose, then turned and ran after them.

They could hear Eliza shouting to them, but they didn't look back.

They ran for quite a ways before Emily stopped, gripping her side. "Wait guys," she huffed. "I have a stitch in my side." She leaned over and took several deep breaths.

"We need to find a place to hide for the night. I don't know if Eliza went to the sheriff or not, but we don't want to stay on the road. Someone might come along and find us."

"Where's dere a place fo us ta stop? Dere's nuffin out here," Mercy said.

"I've heard there's an old abandoned farm out this way. Maybe it's close by. We could stop there and hide for the rest of the night," Thomas said.

"It's too dark to see anything," Emily said. She was finally able to catch her breath, but her side still hurt. "How will we find it?"

"I don't know, but we'll just have to try," said Thomas.

They walked on down the rutted, dusty, dirt road for several minutes when Thomas stopped and squinted off to the right of the road. "Look over there," he said, pointing. "Does that look like an old barn?"

Emily and Mercy both looked in the direction he was pointing, but neither of them could make out any structures in the darkness.

"I's not seein' nuffin over dere," Mercy said. She walked to the edge of the road and peered into the darkness. "It's jus so dark, it's hard ta see."

Ugly walked to the side of the road and began sniffing the air, but didn't seem to smell anything that interested him, so he sat down and began scratching behind his ear.

"Let's walk over there and see," suggested Emily.

They stepped off the road and into a field that was overgrown with tall grass. Ugly jumped up and bounced off into the grass ahead of them.

They had only walked a short distance when Thomas pointed and said, "There! It's an old house!"

"I see it!" said Emily, excitedly.

They were about half way between the road and the house when they heard hoof beats coming down the road.

At the sound of the horses hooves, Ugly appeared out of nowhere next to Emily and hunkered down beside her. He let out a whimper and nudged her hand. She rubbed the top of his head to quiet him down.

"Get down!" Thomas said urgently.

The three of them ducked down behind the tall grass and watched as several men on horseback came trotting up the road. The light from the lanterns they were carrying wasn't bright enough to reach where the three of them were hiding, but they cast enough light to brighten up the whole road.

Emily could see the dark, shadowy faces of about fifteen men. They swung their lanterns around in every direction apparently looking for something. Their muffled voices reached to where the three of them were hiding, but the riders were too far away to be able to distinguish exactly what they were saying.

"It's the sheriff, I think," said Thomas in a very low voice. "Keep still and don't say a word."

Emily and Mercy grabbed each other's hands and crouched even lower in the grass. Ugly snuggled up close to Emily. He seemed to sense the danger, but didn't whimper or whine. Emily patted his head in a comforting gesture and stroked one of his ratty little ears.

As the men came nearer to where the three of them were, their voices grew louder. "Let's check the old farmstead. They couldn't have gotten much farther than this in the dark," they heard one of the men say.

"Mercy let out a small gasp and Emily quickly clamped her hand over her mouth. "Sshhh," she whispered in her ear.

Thomas felt around in the dark until he touched Emily's arm. Grabbing it, he pulled her to her feet and gently tugged as a signal to follow him. She, in turn, clasped Mercy's hand tightly and squeezed. Understanding what was going on, Mercy got to her feet and followed behind them.

The three of them slowly and stealthily tiptoed deeper into the grass, making a wide birth around the house. Ugly followed, sticking closely to Emily's side.

The men had turned their horses off the road into the tall grass heading toward the house. They were not being very quiet as they cut through the field, which made it easy for Thomas, Emily and Mercy to tell exactly where they were. Their lanterns could be seen swinging through the air, casting eerie shadows across the tall grass.

The three of them climbed a small hill that overlooked the back of the house. From their vantage point, they could see that the men had reached the house and were searching it and the area around it. Lantern light spread out in all directions, so they knew the men had split up to search.

Thomas laid down on his stomach and watched the goings on below. Emily and Mercy walked around the hilltop looking for a hiding spot in case the men came up this far. Ugly laid down next to Thomas and seemed content to watch what the men were doing too.

Emily and Mercy were several feet behind Thomas scouring the area when suddenly the ground beneath Emily gave way. She didn't even have time to scream as she fell several feet down into a hole and landed with a thud on her back, knocking the wind out of her.

"Em? Em where'd ya go?" Mercy called to her. Her voice was just barely about a whisper.

Emily could hear her calling, but couldn't seem to get enough air in her lungs to call back. Trying to take deep gulping breaths, she finally managed to suck in a lung full. "Down here, Mercy! I fell in a hole!"

She could hear Mercy shuffling around overhead, but the pit was so dark, she couldn't make out what was around her or above her.

Mercy's voice drifted down to her, "Em? Ya ok?"

She knew Mercy was panicking and was afraid she would give away their hiding location to the men down the hill. "Sshhh, Mercy, it's ok. I'm ok. I just fell into a hole, but I'm not hurt. Go get Thomas!"

She could hear Mercy scrambling away and within a few moments, Thomas's voice could be heard from above her. "Emily, are you ok? What happened?"

"I fell down a hole, Thomas. I'm ok, but I think it's pretty deep."

"Hold on, Emily. We'll try to get you out."

Emily couldn't tell how big the hole was, so she got on her hands and knees and felt her way around the area. She had only taken a few steps when she hit the wall in front of her. Using her hands to feel along the wall, she discovered she was in a circular hole. She still wasn't able to determine how deep it was though.

Standing up on her feet, she reached up as high as she could reach, but couldn't feel the edge of the hole.

Thomas's voice came to her again. "Emily, do you think you could climb out?"

"No, I can't reach the top."

"Just sit tight. The men are leaving. Once they're gone, Mercy and I will head down and see if we can find any rope in the barn or house."

"You can't leave me here!" Emily cried.

"It won't be for long, but we need something to pull you out with."

"No, please don't leave me! I'm scared!"

Emily could hear Thomas and Mercy talking, but couldn't make out what they were saying. She heard Ugly let out whimper now and then.

Suddenly she heard rustling noises coming from overhead. Debris and small pebbles began to fall down on her. "What are you guys doing?"

"Move to one side, Emily. We're going to lower a big branch down into the hole."

Emily quickly moved to one side and flattened herself up against the wall. "What for? What am I supposed to do with a big branch?"

She could hear Thomas and Mercy grunting and groaning about her. Larger pieces of debris began falling down on her and even though she couldn't see it, she knew the branch was being lowered into the pit. One end of it hit the bottom of the hole with a thud.

"Ok, Em," Mercy called down to her. "Sees iffn ya can climb up da branch."

Emily felt around in the dark until she came across the branch. It was a big one alright. She wrapped her hands around it to see if it would be strong enough to hold her weight and discovered it was about as big around as she was.

"I'm going to try to climb up," she called up to them.

Grabbing the branch with both hands, she placed her foot on the bottom of it and lifted herself up. She had to grip the log hard between her hands to keep from falling back down. She moved her other foot up onto the log and pushed herself up. Inch by inch, she slowly hefted herself up to the top. When she reached the opening of the hole, she felt two sets of hands grab her and pull her the rest of the way up. She fell to the ground and rolled over onto her back. She took several deep breaths and exhaled slowly.

"Thank you for not leaving me," she said to them. "That branch was a good idea!"

Ugly began licking her face and whining! Emily started laughing and threw her arms around his neck. "Thanks, Ugly. I'm glad to see you too."

"Sshhh, listen," said Thomas. "I hear someone coming."

They all got quiet and sure enough, the sounds of men talking was getting closer.

"I thought they left," Emily whispered.

"So did I," Thomas answered. "We have to hide."

"Where?" asked Mercy. "Iffn we run, dey gonna hear us. We's got nowhere ta go."

"Hey, I know," Emily said. "Down the hole! We can hide down there. They would never think to look down there."

"Emily, what a great idea," Thomas said. "You and Mercy go down first. I'll grab Ugly and come down behind you. We've got to hurry though. They sound close."

Emily went down first. It was harder going down than it was coming up. Her feet kept slipping and she was having a hard time hanging onto the branch when that happened. She safely reached the bottom though and called for Mercy to come down.

Mercy began the climb down, but lost her grip on the branch and fell backward, landing on her rump at the bottom. She quickly got up and moved out of the way so Thomas could come down. They could hear him talking to Ugly and it didn't sound like Ugly wanted to cooperate.

"Come on, Ugly," Emily called. "You can do it."

"Ya can do it, Ugly," Mercy added. "Come on now, boy."

They could hear Ugly whining and Thomas cooing to him, but they still weren't coming down the branch yet.

"Thomas, hurry!" Emily called.

Ugly let out a yelp, then all of a sudden, he came sliding down the branch with Thomas right behind him.

Ugly landed on all four legs at the bottom. He quickly rushed over to the girls and Emily could feel his whole body shaking. "Just be lucky you didn't fall in the way I did," she told him. "You, at least, got to use the branch."

Thomas reached the bottom and quickly shushed the girls. "They're just outside now," he said, talking about the men.

The three of them huddled up against the wall of the pit and didn't even dare breath. Voices sounded just outside the hole. "They're somewhere around here. I know I heard voices," one of the men said.

"Well, they can't have just disappeared," said another one. "If they had run off, we'd have heard them."

"I'm telling you, I heard them," the first man said.

"Well, if you want to search the woods all night, be my guest, but we're heading back to town. It's been a long night and they're probably long gone by now. I ain't wasting another minute searching for them," said the second man.

The men could be heard shuffling off and soon, the voices faded away.

Emily was too afraid to move in case they were still out there. Mercy slid down the wall and landed on her behind and let out a long sigh.

"Dat was close," she said.

"I think we better just stay in here for the rest of the night," Thomas said. "If they're still out there lying in wait, I don't want to run into them."

"I agree," said Emily. "We're safe in here for now."

Thomas and Emily took a seat on the ground next to Mercy. Ugly curled up on the floor in front of them.

They sat in silence for a long time, listening for the men to return. After awhile, when no noises were heard, they all seemed to relax.

"Well guys, we'd better try to get some sleep. It's probably near to morning and we need to rest as much as we can," Thomas said. "By the way. Where are we going?"

"North," Emily and Mercy both said in unison.

"Ok, North it is," said Thomas, with a big yawn.

Emily pulled the bag off her back and reached inside for the compass. It was still there. She gave it a quick squeeze and said a prayer of thanks that it hadn't been lost.

As she closed her eyes, she pictured home. How she missed it. How she missed her father and Olive. She wondered if she would ever see home again. *No, don't even think that,* she thought to herself. She wasn't about to let herself give in to her fears. Hope was all she had to hold on to. She was so glad she had Mercy, and now, Thomas to go along with her. She couldn't ask for two better friends. In the dark, she grabbed each of their hands and held on to them tightly. Ugly sensed the bond growing between the friends and didn't want to miss out on it, so he crawled up to Emily and laid his head in her lap. "You too, Ugly," she whispered to him. "I'm thankful for you too."

CHAPTER 12

The early morning sun sent beams of light, sprinkled with dust, down into the hole. Emily blinked several times as she sat up and looked around her. She could finally see what was in the hole. Nothing. Just Thomas, Mercy, Ugly and herself. It was just a hole. Barely big enough for the four of them.

Beside her, Mercy stirred and sat up. She rubbed her eyes and yawned. "G'morning, Em."

"Good morning, Mercy."

Ugly stretched out his gangly legs and yawned. He let out a snort and shook his head.

"I agree, Ugly," Emily laughed. "It's time to get up and get out of this hole."

Thomas didn't move, but continued to lightly snore.

"Should we wake him?" Emily asked.

"Les jus gives 'im a few more minutes," Mercy said.

"Yeah, he must be really tired," Emily said. "By the way, Mercy, where did you go when the sheriff caught me? And where did you find Ugly?"

"I dun run off inta da woods a long ways," Mercy said. "I dint know what dey was gonna do wif ya, so I stayed in da woods for a long time. When it was gittin' dark, I come back ta town lookin' fo ya and dat tavern lady found me. She tole me where dey took ya and tole me ta stay wif her till it was time ta go git ya. I dint want ta go wif her, but she tole me she had our dawg and she'd feed me iffn I'd go wif her. I figgered I dint have nuffin ta lose, so I went wif her. She hid me in her room in da upstairs of da tavern and gave me some food and water. She tole me she feeled real bad 'bout turnin' us in, but she tot she was doin' da right ting. She tole me dat she saw us go inta da liv'ry stable and saw us up in da hay loft. She nabbed Ugly from da barn and took 'im ta her place fo da night, hopin' we'd go lookin' fo 'im and den she could turn us over ta da sheriff. But in da mornin' when da sheriff nabbed ya, she knowed she don da wrong ting, so she wanted ta help me out. So when it got dark, I lef her place and went ta da orphanage. I dint know where ya was so I just started trowing rocks at da house and hoped ya knowed it was me and come ta da winder. It worked."

"How did you get Ugly to dig the hole under the fence?" Emily asked.

"I dint. He don dat on his own."

Emily looked down at Ugly who had laid his head in her lap again. She rubbed behind his ears and gave him a little scratch. "You really are a good dog, aren't you?" He thumped his tail on the ground and let out a little whine.

At the sound, Thomas roused from his sleeping and sat up.

"Good morning, girls," he said with a big yawn.

"Good morning, Thomas," Emily said.

"G'mornin'," said Mercy.

Now that Thomas was awake, they began to climb out of the hole. Ugly raced up the branch before everyone else and stood at the top yipping at them to follow him. One by one, they climbed out of the hole and looked around.

The sky was a clear blue, but fluffy white clouds were beginning to form. The smell of rain was in the air and a cool breeze began to ruffle the leaves on the trees.

"I think it's going to rain," said Thomas. "We need to head to the house."

"But what if those men come back?" Emily asked.

"They already searched it. I doubt if they'll come back."

"I's all fo headin' ta da house. I's not really wantin' ta get all wet," Mercy said.

They made their way down the hill to the house. It started to sprinkle just as they reached the back porch.

The house was in poor shape. The roof sagged and several of the floorboards on the porch were rotted through. The white, clapboard siding was peeling and there were holes in many of the slats.

They stepped up onto the crumbling porch and entered the house through a door that was barely hanging by it's hinges.

Suddenly the sky opened up and rain poured down. Thunder rumbled and lightning flashed across the darkening sky.

Rain dripped down on them from holes in the roof as they made their way through the house looking for a dry spot to wait out the storm.

Entering the main living area, they noticed it was the driest room they had come across.

Taking a seat on the floor in front of the fireplace, the three of them settled in. Ugly pranced around the room, unhappy to be stuck inside. He finally settled himself down next to Thomas and fell asleep.

"So," Thomas said. "Tell me what's going on with you two. How did you get down here and where are you headed?"

Emily shifted herself to face him and began to tell him the whole story up to the point where she met him at the orphanage.

"Wow," Thomas said. "So you guys are trying to get back up North. How do you plan on doing that? You can't possibly walk the whole way. How do you even know where you're going?

"I'll show you," Emily said. She pulled the compass out of the bag and handed it to him. "It's a compass that Mary gave us."

"So, this will point North and if you follow it, you will eventually find home?"

"Well, yes," Emily said. "I know it'll take us a long time, but we'll make it one way or another."

"That's a long way away. How are you going to find food? Or a place to sleep at night?"

We's bin findin' food here an dere along da way. We sleeps wherever we can fine a spot to lay our heads down."

"Thomas," Emily began. "You are planning to come with us, aren't you?"

"Well, I don't have anywhere else to go, so I suppose so. I can't stay around here. I'll just end up in the orphanage again."

"Yay!" Emily exclaimed. She leaned over and gave him a quick hug. "You guys will live with me from now on. I just know my father will take you in."

"Umm, Em?" Mercy said. "I don know iffn he'll want me. I's not white. He prolly won't want no blackie in 'is house."

"You don't know my father then," Emily said. "He isn't like that. You'll be welcome there, I promise."

Mercy looked uncertainly at her, but didn't say anything more.

"We need to figure out what our next plan is if we're going to be hitting the road once the rain stops," said Thomas.

"We'll just stick to the road for awhile and see where it goes," Emily said.

"We can't do that," Thomas said. "What if those men come along again?"

"We can stay in da woods den," Mercy said. "We's traveled mos' of da way in da woods."

Ugly jerked his head up and let out a long whine. His ears suddenly laid back on his head and a deep growl rumbled out of his throat.

Before any one of them could react, a tall figure stepped into the doorway of the room.

Emily gasped and jumped to her feet. Thomas grabbed Ugly by the scruff of the neck, while Mercy sat there looking at the newcomer with her mouth wide open.

"Maybe I can help," said the person who was standing in the doorway. She stepped into the room from the shadows. It was the lady from the tavern.

"What are you doing here?" Emily demanded. "Did you come to take us back to the orphanage?"

"No, I came to help you," the tavern lady said. "By the way, my name is Bessie. What are you boys names, if you don't mind?"

Emily looked at her dumbfounded for a moment before she could speak. She removed the cap from her head and let her long braid fall down her back. Pointing at Mercy, she said, "We aren't boys. My name is Emily and this is Mercy. This here is Thomas." She motioned with her head toward Thomas as she introduced him.

"Well, well, well now," Bessie said. "I never figured you for girls, what with those outfits and all." She looked Emily and Mercy over from head to toe.

"How can ya hep us?" Mercy asked her. "Did ya brin' us sum food?"

"As a matter of fact, I did. I left it out in the wagon though. We'll have to go get it once the rain stops."

"How did you know we were here? Are you helping the sheriff?" Thomas asked suspiciously.

"No, young man," Bessie said. "I knew this was the only place between here and the next town. The only real place that you could possibly be hiding. The sheriff knew that too. That's why he came out here last night looking for you."

"How are you going to help us?" Emily asked her.

"The next town is a long way off. I figured I could hide you in the back of my wagon and take you at least as far as the town. I brought some food and water for you, as well. I know it doesn't do much to get you home, but it's all I can do. I feel real bad about turning you into the sheriff. I thought I was helping, but I know now, it was the wrong thing to do. So I want to make it up to you, if you'll let me," Bessie told them.

"We need to discuss this among the three of us. Could you give us a minute, please?" Emily asked her.

"Of course," Bessie said. She stepped out of the room while Thomas, Emily and Mercy put their heads together. Ugly tried squeezing in the middle of them, but Emily pushed him away, so he followed Bessie out of the room.

"What do you guys think?" Thomas asked. "Do you think we can trust her?"

"Well, she did hep me affer Em was taken ta da orphanage," Mercy reminded them.

"I still don't trust her," Emily said. "But I guess Mercy is right. She did help her, so maybe she will help us now. I just don't want to end up back at the orphanage again."

"Ok, so we vote," said Thomas. "All in favor of letting her help us, say I."

"I," said Mercy.

Emily hesitated a moment, then reluctantly said, "I."

"Ok, then," Thomas said. "We all agree. Let's call her back in."

When Bessie rejoined them in the room, they told her they would accept her help.

"I'm so glad," she said. "I want to make up for turning you in, so thank you."

"When do you want to leave?" Thomas asked her.

"Let's wait till the rain passes. I don't think the sheriff will be coming around again, but I think it's best to leave as soon as possible, just in case."

When the rain slowed down for a bit, Bessie had Thomas run out to her wagon that she had pulled into the barn to hide it from any passersby and bring in a basket of food she had stashed under the seat.

They all sat in a circle in the middle of the room and enjoyed cold chicken, dried bread, a chunk of cheese and fresh apples. Ugly was given the chicken scraps and she had packed a few leftovers from the tavern for him.

As they sat around eating their lunch, Emily told the story to Bessie of how they all ended up where they were. Bessie listened intently to the whole story. Once Emily had finished the tale, Bessie let out a low whistle.

"Do you know who those men are? Mr. Guthrie and Mr. Cordell? Could you give me descriptions of them and where you think they were headed. That is information that I can pass along to the sheriff and he can pass it on to other towns as well. What those men are doing is not right and they need to be stopped."

Emily and Mercy gave her the best descriptions they could of the men and told her about the auction somewhere in South Carolina that they were taking the girls to.

"Thank you," Bessie said. "I will see what I can do to pass the word along."

The rain poured down most of the day. It finally began to let up just as the sun was setting. Darkness began to creep into the house, casting long shadows in the corners and making it hard to see around the room.

When they could no longer hear the rain hitting the roof, Bessie announced it was time to go.

"Best get on the road now," she said. "The rain's about stopped."

They packed up the leftover food into the basket and stepped out into the cool evening. The rain had lowered the temperatures and a slight chill filled the air.

They walked the short distance to the barn and found Bessie's wagon right where she said it would be. Two large bay stallions were harnessed to the front of it and a large canvas tarp was spread out over the back.

Bessie pulled the tarp back and revealed a pallet made of several blankets and a couple of pillows.

"I thought you would be more comfortable on the blankets then on the wooden floor of the wagon," she told them. "We have a long ride to the next town, so I wanted you to be comfortable."

Emily was impressed at her thoughtfulness. She gave her a quick hug around her middle.

"How long will it take to get to the town," Thomas asked.

"It'll take till morning at least," Bessie said. "You'll be happy to know that the town is in North Carolina, so you'll be one state closer to home."

Emily and Mercy giggled and jumped up and down, holding each other's hands.

Ugly didn't wait for them to crawl into the wagon. He jumped up into the back of it and curled up near the front, under the seat.

"Well, I guess he's ready to go," Bessie said.

Thomas helped Emily and Mercy up into the wagon, then he hoisted himself up in. They all moved to the front of the wagon and got comfortable under the tarp.

"Make yourselves comfortable and try to get some sleep. I'll wake you when we get close to the town. Whatever you do though, don't make any noise."

The three of them promised they wouldn't and pulled the tarp up over their heads. Ugly didn't like being under the tarp, so he wriggled his way out from under it and jumped up onto the seat next to Bessie.

"I guess you'll be my sidekick," Bessie told him.

She maneuvered the horses and wagon out of the barn and steered them toward the road.

Once they were on the road, the wagon jostled and bounced along the rutted, dirt tracks, rocking the three of them as they lay in the back.

It was completely dark now. Under the tarp was warm and the constant rocking of the wagon was lulling Emily to sleep. She didn't want to go to sleep yet. She was still worried that Bessie might not really be helping them, but taking them back to town.

At one point, she lifted the tarp up and poked her head out to look around. The road was lined with tall, thickly leafed trees that were covered in a sea foam colored moss. The storm clouds had passed and the night sky was ablaze with a million stars.

The moon hung high in the sky and a cool breeze blew across her face. It was a beautiful night.

After looking around for several more minutes, Emily settled back down in the wagon and curled up next to Mercy. Thomas was on the other side of Mercy, snoring softly.

"We's gonna make it home, Em," Mercy whispered in the darkness.

"I sure hope so, Mercy."

"Does ya really tink yor daddy will allow me ta stay wif ya?"

"Yes, I do. He is a really nice man and he wouldn't turn you away just because your skin is a different color."

"How ya know dat fo sho?"

"Because Olive is black."

"She is?"

"Yes. And Father allows her to stay with us."

"Is her a slave?"

"No, she's our housekeeper, cook and also my nanny. She's part of our family."

"Mebbe I can has a job too den and be a part a yo family."

"You will be my sister, Mercy. You won't need a job."

"I don tink dat's how it works, Em."

"We'll see."

Emily could feel Mercy shaking her head, but she didn't say anything more.

CHAPTER 13

Sometime in the early morning, Bessie roused the kids from their sleep. She reached back and lifted the tarp, looking down at them. "Time to wake up," she said. "We're almost there."

Emily stuck her head out from under the tarp and looked around. The trees were thinning out and the sun was beginning to rise over the horizon.

"Stay under the tarp till I tell you to come out. I want to make sure it's safe first," Bessie told them.

Emily ducked back under the tarp and pulled it securely around her.

The wagon bumped along for several more minutes before it came to a stop. Emily wanted to peek out again, but Mercy grabbed her arm. "Don lift da cover," she said. "Some'un might sees ya. Jus wait fo Bessie."

"Sshhh," said Thomas. "Someone might hear you."

The tarp was suddenly thrown back and Bessie looked down at them smiling. "It's all clear," she said.

Emily jumped up and was out of the wagon before the other two even sat up. She straightened her clothes and looked around.

The town was considerably larger than the one they had come from. The street was bustling with people and horses. Buggies rushed past them in both directions.

When they had all climbed down from the wagon, Bessie led them across the street to the mercantile. Ugly started to followed them, but then turned and trotted off down the street.

Stopping just outside the door to the store, Bessie turned to them and said. "I need to pick up a few supplies to take back with me. I know the gentleman who owns this store, so I'm going to ask him for a few extra tidbits for you for your journey."

They entered the store and Bessie went straight to the counter. An older gentleman stepped up to the counter and immediately greeted her.

"Ah, Miss Bessie," he said. "It's so good to see you again. It's been ages." He picked up her hand and kissed the back of it.

"It's good to see you again too, Sam," she said. She seemed genuinely pleased to see him. She smiled a wide smile and ducked her head slightly to one side as if she was shy.

"What can I do for you this fine morning," Sam asked her.

"I need my usual supplies and…" she leaned closer to him. "I need a few extras for the kids." She whispered the last part and nodded her head toward Emily, Mercy and Thomas.

"Please step into the back with me," he said, pulling back a curtain that separated the front store room from his living quarters.

Bessie motioned for the three of them to follow her. They quickly stepped behind the curtain and Sam dropped it back down into place.

"Now, tell me what's going on," he said calmly to Bessie. She quickly explained the circumstances while Sam rubbed his jaw and make an occasional "hhmmm" sound.

"So, there are men out looking for the two girls?" he asked. "Give me their descriptions and names and I'll post fliers in the windows. That way, anyone who sees them can notify the sheriff. Once I get your supplies all rounded up, I'll run over to his office and inform him at once as to what's going on."

"Thank you, Sam," Bessie said.

"Now, let's go get those supplies," Sam said.

They entered the store area again and Sam rushed around gathering up the supplies Bessie had asked for.

Once all the supplies were gathered, Thomas helped Sam load them into the back of Bessie's wagon.

"I have one more thing that I think I can do to help these young folks out," Sam told Bessie as he helped her up onto the seat of her wagon.

"What is it, Sam?" Bessie asked.

"Do you remember old Mrs. Thorne?"

"Aahhh, yes, of course. Why didn't I think of that?" Bessie replied.

"Who's Mrs. Thorne," Emily asked.

"She's an old widow who lives up in the mountains. She comes down once a month for supplies and tomorrow is her normal day to come. She's been looking for someone to help her with some work around her place. You see, she's old and can't do a lot of the work that needs done around there. Every month she comes into town and asks around to see if she can find someone she can hire to work for her. I think the three of you are exactly what she needs. And you need her. She'll pay you for your work and she'll give you a place to stay. Winter will be here before you know it and you don't want to be traveling through the mountains in the winter. It's the perfect solution for you and her," Sam explained.

Thomas looked at Emily and Mercy. "What do you think?"

"I think it's a great idea," Emily said. "We could stay with her through the winter and then head out again come spring. We sure could use the money too. We'll need it for food and such."

Mercy remained quiet. Emily and Thomas looked to her for her answer, but she just slowly shook her head.

"What is it, Mercy?" Emily asked her.

"Dat's great fo da two of yuns, but wha 'bout me? She ain't gonna want no blackie."

"Well, you would be wrong there, Mercy," Bessie said. "Mrs. Thorne won't care what color your skin is."

"She won't?" Mercy asked, skeptically.

"She sure won't. You see, she's as blind as a bat," Sam laughed. "She won't know what color you were, and truth be told, she wouldn't care. She'll just be glad for the help."

A huge smile crossed Mercy's face. "Den I's all fo it."

"Bessie, before you go, why don't you let me take you and these kids down to the restaurant and let me buy you all something to eat," Sam said.

Bessie blushed and nodded. Turning to the kids, she asked, "Is that alright with you guys?"

Emily nodded excitedly. She hadn't been to a restaurant since her father had taken her when she was little. Olive was such a good cook, they almost always ate at home.

Thomas and Mercy gave their consent as well. They walked as a group down the boardwalk to the restaurant. Emily saw that it was named Annie's. She liked the name and hoped she liked the food just as well.

It was still early morning, so the restaurant was serving breakfast. As they pulled up chairs at a table in the corner overlooking the street, Sam suddenly jumped up and excused himself. They all watched as he made his way across the room and approached a man wearing a badge.

"That must be the sheriff," Thomas said.

"I'm so glad he's telling him about Mr. Guthrie and Mr. Cordell," Emily said.

"Sam is a very good man," Bessie said. "He will do whatever he can to help."

Emily looked at Bessie and saw the wide smile that spread across her face.

"You like him, don't you?" she asked Bessie.

Bessie blushed a deep pink. She quietly nodded her head. "Yes, very much so."

"Why aren't you two married then?" Emily asked.

"We were engaged a long time ago, but Sam's mama didn't like me very much. She forbade him to marry me. I've never stopped loving him though."

"How sad," Thomas said. "Why didn't his mother like you?"

"She didn't think I was the right woman for her son. I was a bit younger than Sam and I was born into a poor family. She wanted him to marry someone more proper, I guess. He eventually married another woman and I moved to another town." There was a deep sadness in her eyes as she spoke. Emily's heart broke for her.

"Where is his wife now?" Thomas asked.

"She passed away a few years ago," Bessie said.

"Well then, why don't you marry him now?" Emily asked.

"It's too late for that," Bessie said, sadly. "Please, no more talk of Sam. My heart can't take it."

They all got quiet as Sam walked back to their table. "Well, the sheriff is now aware of the men who kidnapped you and will be keeping his eye out for them. Hopefully, they won't come this way, but if they do, we'll catch them," he said. He looked around the table at each one of them and asked, "Why all the long faces? What's happened?"

"We's jus sad dat yo an' Bessie can't be ta'gether," Mercy said.

"What?" he asked looking at Bessie. "You still feel that way about me? Even after all this time?"

Bessie looked down at the table and nodded.

"Well, I'll be," Sam said, slowly. "Bessie, look at me."

She lifted her head and looked at him, a small tear in the corner of her eye.

"Bessie, I still love you too," he said. "I always have. I only married Grace to make Mama happy, but they're both gone now. I had no idea you still had feelings for me. I thought you had moved on long ago."

"Sam, I never stopped loving you. Why do you think I never married? I could never love anyone but you."

"Oh Bessie," Sam said. "I'm so sorry I hurt you all those years ago. If I could go back and do it again, it would have been you I would have married."

"It was a long time ago," Bessie said, softly. "It doesn't matter now."

Sam got out of his chair and knelt down on the floor beside Bessie. Taking her hand in his, he asked, "Bessie Mae Holston, will you marry me and make me the happiest man in the world?"

Emily let out a loud gasp and clamped her hand over her mouth. Thomas and Mercy just stared at them with their mouths wide open.

"Oh yes, Sam," Bessie said barely above a whisper. "Yes."

Sam jumped up off the floor and grabbed Bessie's hands and pulled her up out of her chair. Planting a big kiss on her lips, he pulled her into a hug and spun her around.

Emily, Mercy and Thomas began to cheer.

"Let's do it today," Sam said. "Why wait? We can ask Reverend Miles to do it this afternoon."

Bessie had tears running down her cheeks, but she was smiling. "The kids can be our witnesses. Right kids?"

"Yes," said Emily.

"It would be my pleasure," Thomas said.

"I'd be glad ta do it," Mercy said.

Bessie hugged each one of them. "Thank you," she said. "This is the best day of my life."

They ordered their breakfast and when the eggs, bacon and toast arrived, they all ate hungrily.

When they were done, Sam and Bessie took off for the church building looking for Reverend Miles, while Thomas, Emily and Mercy walked around town.

Every once in awhile, they caught sight of Ugly exploring his way around. He would dart in and out of alleyways and disappear behind buildings only to come out from around the other side. They didn't bother to try to get him to stay with them. He was having fun and so they let him be.

As the three of them walked past the saloon, none of them noticed the man peering at them from behind the swinging door. They also didn't notice when he silently pushed the door open and stepped out onto the boardwalk behind them.

CHAPTER 14

As the day wore on, Emily, Thomas and Mercy were growing tired of walking around the dusty streets. They had seen every inch of the town and were ready for a nice shady place to sit down and rest and wait for the wedding ceremony that was to take place in a couple of hours.

As they came to the edge of town, a tall tree stood off to the side of the road. Its large branches were heavy with leaves and the shade under it was a welcome sight.

As they started to pass by the last building on the street, Emily thought she saw a man duck down the alley between it and the building beside it. She looked back, but didn't see anyone. She shrugged it off and kept walking.

When they reached the tree, they sat down under it and leaned back against the trunk, enjoying the coolness of the shade.

Ugly had finally joined them again. He plopped himself down on the ground in front of them and began to doze. He had spent the entire day running around the town and had worn himself out. He started to snore as the three kids began to discuss the day.

"I think it's exciting that we'll be in a wedding," Emily said.

"I agree," said Thomas. "I didn't see that coming."

"Did ya see Bessie's dress? She gonna look so good fo Sam," Mercy said.

They had passed by the mercantile earlier in the day and through the window, saw Bessie and Sam picking out their outfits for the wedding. They had stopped in to see if there was anything they could do to help, but Bessie told them she and Sam had it all taken care of and to just make sure they were at the church at sundown. So the three of them continued their exploration of the town until they eventually stopped at the tree.

"It was nice of Reverend Miles to let us sleep in the church tonight," Emily said. "I didn't want to have to sleep in the back of the wagon again. My back is sore from all the bumps."

"Since Bessie's gonna be wif Sam at 'is house tonight, we's gonna be in dere all alone. I's never bin in a church a'fore."

"Never?" Thomas asked.

"Nope," Mercy said. "I's heared dey's real nice, doe."

"You'll find out soon enough," Emily said. "We probably better head that way soon. We don't want to be late."

"It's still a couple of hours off," said Thomas. "Let's just rest here a bit longer. I'm hot and tired."

"We can stay a few more minutes, but then we need to go. The church is on the other end of town and it will take us a few minutes to get there. The streets are still packed with so many people and horses."

Mercy gazed down the street that ran through the middle of the town. The sun was sitting low in the sky, but it would still be a couple of hours before it got dark. Her gaze traveled along the buildings until she caught sight of something that made her take a second look.

"Dos ya guys see dat man standin' b'tween dem buildins right dere," she said, pointing to the buildings that Emily had seen the man dart between just a short time ago.

Emily and Thomas looked to where she was pointing, but the man had ducked back out of sight.

"I don't see anyone," Thomas said.

Emily was still staring at the spot. A creepy feeling was crawling up her spine. "I thought I saw someone standing between those buildings when we walked past awhile ago."

"Maybe it's just one of the townsfolk," Thomas suggested.

"Maybe, but why would he be hiding between buildings watching us?" Emily asked. "I don't like this. Let's get to the church and find Bessie and Sam."

They got up and dusted the grass off their clothes. Keeping their eyes on the spot where Mercy had seen the man, they quickly started on their way down the street to the far end where the church sat.

Ugly decided not to follow them to the church, but instead, turned back toward the restaurant to see if he could beg some food scraps from the cooks at the back door. Emily, Mercy and Thomas went on without him.

The church was a small, white building with a large bell tucked neatly into the bell tower. The front doors were red and above the door was a sign that read, *Christ's Church, Est. 1824.*

Climbing the steps to the front door, Mercy paused and looked up at the sign. Emily and Thomas stopped right behind her.

"What's wrong, Mercy?" Emily asked. "Go on in."

"I's not sho I can," Mercy said.

"Why not?" Thomas asked.

"It's a white folks church," Mercy said, taking a step back. "I'd git inta lots of trouble iffn I step a foot in dat place."

"You'll be sleeping in here later," Emily said. "You must be allowed in."

"Dat'll be at night when no un would see me go in. Dis is still durin' da day when ever'body would see me."

About that time, the door swung open and a tall, thin man wearing a black robe stepped out. He looked at the three of them and smiled.

"You must be Thomas, Emily and Mercy," he said. "Come on in."

"Sir," Mercy began. "I's not allowed in dere."

"Well, for Heaven's sake, why not, child?" the Reverend Miles asked.

"Cause I's a colored child," Mercy said.

"Well, in this church, God's church, everyone is welcome, no matter your skin color."

Mercy stared at him wide eyed. "We's still in da souf right?"

Reverend Miles laughed and put his hand on Mercy's shoulder. "Yes indeed, but this town isn't like most Southern towns. We don't agree with the whole slavery thing and we don't abide by those rules. It has caused us some trouble, but we won't be changing our ways. Now come on in and let's get you kids ready for the wedding."

Mercy looked over her shoulder at Emily and Thomas and shrugged. Stepping through the doors into the church, she was overwhelmed with the beauty she saw. Stained glass windows with depictions of Jesus, the cross and a dove covered the front of the building. Down the sides, long, narrow windows were spaced every few feet apart. Wooden pews glistened with a fresh coat of wax and a long red floor runner ran the length of the building from the door to the pulpit. The church was immaculately clean and candles had been lit on a stand up in the front. The smell of incense filled the whole room.

"Ooohhhhh my," Mercy whispered. "I's never seen no place purtier dan dis."

Emily and Thomas followed her in and looked around.

"Yes, it is very beautiful," Emily said. "The church my father took me to was a lot bigger than this one, but it wasn't nearly as beautiful."

The three of them walked to the front of the room and took a seat on the front pew.

Reverend Miles walked into a doorway that led off the back of the room. He turned to them and said, "I'll be right back. I'm just going to let Bessie and Sam know you're here." He disappeared behind the door, leaving the three of them sitting there alone.

Everything was very still and quiet. No noises came from the back where the Reverend had gone. They were the only people in there.

Emily looked around the room admiring all the beautiful splotches of color that the stained glass windows were creating as the sun shined through them. Her eyes fell on one of the side windows and her heart stopped.

Looking in at them through the window was none other than Mr. Guthrie.

Emily let out a scream and jumped up out of her seat.

Thomas and Mercy were startled by her scream and jumped up as well.

"Emily, what's wrong?" Thomas asked, looking around.

"Mr. Guthrie," Emily said. "He was watching us through that window." She was pointing at the window she had seen his face in, but he was no longer there.

"Are ya sho, Em?" Mercy asked her.

"Yes, I saw him very plainly," Emily said. "He was right there."

Reverend Miles and Bessie came out of the door that Reverend Miles had entered just moments before.

"What's going on out here?" Bessie asked. "We heard you scream."

"Mr. Guthrie was in the window," Emily said. She had started to tremble and her stomach was in knots.

"Mr. Guthrie?" Bessie asked. "You mean the man who kidnapped you?"

"Yes," Emily said. "He was watching us through that window." She pointed again to the window she had seen him in.

Everyone turned to look at the window again, but Mr. Guthrie was not there.

"Are you sure it was Mr. Guthrie?" Bessie asked.

"Yes, yes, yes," Emily said, frustrated. "I would know him anywhere. What a horrid man."

Bessie looked at Reverend Miles and said, "Go get the sheriff please."

Reverend Miles nodded his head and took off out the front door.

"Now listen, children," Bessie said. "If he is out there, you'll be safe in here with us. We won't let him or anyone else in here. The sheriff already knows about this situation and if Mr. Guthrie is out there, he will be caught and put in jail."

The three of them nodded, but Emily kept glancing back at the window. She reached over and grabbed Mercy's hand and squeezed it.

"Mercy, we can't go back with Mr. Guthrie," she said softly in Mercy's ear. "He'll kill us."

"I knows dat, Em," Mercy said. "We's gotta jus stay here wif Bessie and wait fo da sheriff."

Thomas watched the girls holding hands and a sudden fierce need to protect them came over him. He didn't know what all they had endured at Mr. Guthrie's hands, but by the looks on their faces, he knew it wasn't good. Walking over to them, he put his arms around them both. "No one is going to hurt you as long as I'm here," he said to them. "No one."

Emily leaned in to him and laid her head on his shoulder. She was starting to think of him as a brother and her affection for him was growing fast.

Bessie sat with them until the sheriff arrived with Reverend Miles. Emily explained to him what she saw and that they had felt like someone was following them and watching them earlier in the day as well.

The sheriff left them in the church as he went outside to look around. After several minutes, he came back in and assured them that there was no one out there.

"I'll keep an eye out to make sure he doesn't return, but for now, you're all safe in here with the reverend, Bessie and Sam. If I see or hear anything, I'll let you know." With that, he left the church and headed back to his office down the street.

"Well, it's time to get ready for a wedding," Reverend Miles said, clapping his hands together.

"Girls, why don't you come with me and get cleaned up," Bessie said. "Thomas, you follow the reverend and he'll take you back to Sam where you can get cleaned up."

Emily and Mercy followed Bessie through the door in the back and Thomas followed Reverend Miles through the door and down a short hallway to where Sam was.

The small room where Bessie was getting ready was windowless, which made Emily feel safer. No windows meant no Mr. Guthrie looking in on them.

Bessie indicated a washstand in the corner where a bowl of water and a small slither of soap sat, along with a dingy towel. "Just wash up as best you can and then we'll do something with your hair," she told Emily and Mercy.

Emily removed the muslin top and began rubbing the soap between her hands. Once they were good and lathered, she proceeded to rub over her face, neck and arms. She rinsed off in the basin of water and dried herself on the towel.

Mercy repeated what Emily had done and soon, both girls were dust free and smelled faintly of roses from the soap.

Bessie had slipped into her blue dress and brushed out her long hair. Twisting it into a bun, she secured it on top of her head. She turned to Emily and looked admiringly at her long braid.

"Emily," she said. "Let's loosen that braid and give your hair a good brushing. I bet you have beautiful hair."

"Yes, ma'am," Emily said. "My father always said my hair was my glory." She quickly removed the braid and began to unweave the strands. Her hair fell in long rivulets of curls down her back. Bessie grabbed up her brush and began to use long strokes to work out any knots and tangles.

Mercy watched Bessie brushing out Emily's hair and wished she had hair like that. She reached up and touched her spiky strands and let out a long sigh.

"Mercy, I know what you're thinking," Bessie said. "But you have to know that God made you beautiful just the way you are. Your hair may be stiff and course, but it's beautiful none the less."

"Tank ya, ma'am," Mercy said. She quit fussing with her spikes and watched as Bessie twisted Emily's hair up into a tight bun and fastened it to her head with pins.

"I wish I had dresses for you two, but I guess those boy's clothes will just have to do," Bessie sighed.

Emily and Mercy looked at each other and giggled. They much preferred the boy's clothes, but they didn't bother telling Bessie that.

A knock sounded at the door and Reverend Miles voice could be heard on the other side. "It's about time, ladies," he said.

"Coming," Bessie called to him. She gave the girls one last appraising look and asked, "Alright, girls, are you ready?"

"Yes, ma'am," said Emily. Her cheeks were pink from the scrubbing and her hair was piled high on her head. She was a bit nervous for Thomas to see her this way, but she didn't understand why. He wasn't going to care how she looked, was he?

Mercy followed behind Emily as they walked out into the main part of the church. She was still a bit uncomfortable being in there, but she was very glad to be a part of Bessie's wedding. She was just glad that Thomas and Emily were there with her.

Taking a seat on the front pew, Emily looked around at all the windows again. But no Mr. Guthrie. She turned back around when Thomas and Reverend Miles walked into the room. Thomas took a seat next to Mercy, while Reverend Miles walked behind the pulpit and laid his Bible down.

Emily glanced down the pew at Thomas. He was scrubbed clean and his clothing had been shaken out to remove the dust. She thought he looked a bit older somehow, but shook the thought from her head.

Everyone's eyes turned when Sam and Bessie stepped out from the back door into the main room. They walked over to stand in front of Reverend Miles.

Emily thought she had never seen a more beautiful wedding. Sam and Bessie held hands through the whole ceremony and when Reverend Miles told Sam to kiss his bride, Emily, Mercy and Thomas all stood up and clapped.

When the ceremony was over, Emily, Mercy and Thomas congratulated the couple and watched them head for the door.

"Wait," said Emily. "What about us?"

Bessie turned back to her and rushed over and gave her and the other two quick hugs. "You guys will be just fine here with Reverend Miles. The sheriff is keeping an eye on things. Everything will be ok. Sam and I are going home for the night, but I'll come see you tomorrow before you leave with Mrs. Thorne."

Emily watched them leave the church with a dabble of fear running up her spine. She knew why she was afraid. Mr. Guthrie was out there somewhere. How would Reverend Miles keep them safe if Mr. Guthrie decided to come in and take them? She scanned the room, but couldn't find a place that would be suitable to hide in. It was just an open room with a few pews and a pulpit.

Disheartened, she turned to Mercy and Thomas. "We need to keep our eyes open tonight. Mr. Guthrie knows we are in here."

"Maybe we need to take turns keeping watch," Thomas said.

"Good idee," said Mercy. "I's gonna take da firs' watch den."

"I'll take the second," Emily said.

"I guess I'll take the last," Thomas said. "If either of you hear or see anything, wake me up."

"Wha's we gonna do iffn sumpin does happen?"

"Run like our lives depend on it," Emily said. "Cause they do."

Reverend Miles made a couple of pallets on the floor at the front of the church for them. One for the girls on one side of the church and another one for Thomas on the other side of the church. Once he saw that they were settled down and ready for bed, he left them to head back to his own chambers.

The only light was from the candles on the stand. Emily had asked Reverend Miles not to blow them out when he left for the evening. The yellow, flickering glow from them cast long, deep shadows around the room. Reverend Miles informed them that he could not lock the front door because the building was left open to all who would want to come in and spend time with the Lord. This revelation frightened

Emily. It meant that if Mr. Guthrie wanted to come in, he could just walk right through the front door.

Mercy took a seat on the pew and turned sideways so she could watch the whole room. Emily pulled her pallet as close to Mercy as she could get, but she was still very scared. Looking over through the dim candlelight, she saw that Thomas was sitting up on his pallet looking back at her.

"Thomas," she whispered loudly to him. "Come over here with us. I'm scared."

He scrambled around gathering up his pallet and brought it over, laying it out on the floor next to hers.

"Thank you," he said. "I wasn't real happy about sleeping over there all by myself."

"I didn't like it much either. We're used to sleeping together and I feel safer that way."

"I don't think the reverend would be too happy about it though. He probably feels it's improper. That's why he put me clear over there," Thomas said.

"Well, I don't care if he likes it or not," Emily said. She curled up on her pallet facing him.

Mercy watched the two of them but didn't say anything. She noticed that Emily was starting to act a little weird around Thomas, but didn't understand why. She shook her head to clear it and went back to watching the room.

The night wore on uneventfully. Mercy's eyes began to sag and her head would occasionally drop to her chest and she would jerk it up as her eyes flew open. The smoke from the candles was beginning to burn her throat and she let out a little cough.

Emily stirred and sat up. "Mercy, it's time for you to get some sleep. I'll take over now."

Mercy didn't argue and slipped off the pew and onto her pallet.

Emily stood up and stretched. Letting out a big yawn, she took Mercy's place on the pew. She gazed around the darkened room, but all seemed still and quiet. She sat there for a long time listening for any noise, but the only thing she heard was Thomas's gentle snoring.

Sometime later, as her eyes began to droop and her mind was becoming fuddled, something jolted her awake. Listening intently, she heard it again. A soft scraping noise. Then soft thuds. Footsteps. She was hearing footsteps coming down the aisle toward her.

CHAPTER 15

Emily sat bolt upright, fear gripping her so tight she could hardly breathe. The footsteps had stopped, then suddenly a soft whimper.

Emily let out the breath she was holding and relaxed her shoulders. "Ugly," she called. "Come on, boy."

Ugly bolted the rest of the way down the aisle to where she was sitting. He jumped up next to her and laid down. Relief flooded over her as she petted his head and rubbed behind his ears. "You really scared me," she told him. "I thought you were Mr. Guthrie."

She glanced down at Thomas and Mercy and saw that they were still sleeping. She leaned back on the arm of the pew and swept her gaze around the room. For an instant, she thought she saw a shadow move in the far back corner. Straining her eyes, she stared at the corner for several moments, but didn't see anything.

She dropped her gaze to where Thomas and Mercy lay sleeping. Ugly's appearance had not woken them up. She figured she'd let them sleep awhile longer before waking Thomas for his turn to keep watch.

Ugly suddenly sat up and turned his attention to the far corner where, just moments ago, Emily thought she had seen something. His ears laid back on his head and he let out a long, deep growl. The hair on the back of Emily's neck stood up.

"What is it, boy?" she asked.

Ugly jumped down from the pew and stepped out into the aisle facing the main door. Suddenly, his low growl turned into a sharp, loud bark.

Emily jumped up from her seat. At the same time, Thomas and Mercy woke up from all the commotion.

"Who's there?" Emily called out.

The door to the church slammed shut.

Thomas and Mercy, now fully awake, went to stand beside her. Ugly began barking in earnest, but didn't move from his spot.

"You thought you were going to get away from me, didn't you?" a deep, growling voice said to them from near the door.

Emily gasped as she realized it was Mr. Guthrie. "The sheriff knows you're here," she told him.

"He didn't search the area real well when you told him you saw me at the window. I was hiding under the church, but he never bothered to look there." Mr. Guthrie told them.

"Why can't you just leave us alone?" Emily cried.

"You know too much. You could end up causing me a lot of grief. Besides, nobody gets away from me and lives to tell about it."

"We won't tell anyone. Just leave us alone," Emily said.

"Too late for that now, ain't it? The sheriff already knows and I'll bet he'll get the word around about me soon enough."

"If you leave now, we won't tell him you were here," Thomas said.

"Who are you?" Mr. Guthrie snarled.

"That doesn't matter," Thomas said.

"Just one more kid for me to make money off of," Mr. Guthrie said.

Ugly suddenly leaped at Mr. Guthrie, grabbing him by the leg and sinking his teeth deep into his calf. Mr. Guthrie let out a scream and kicked Ugly hard in the ribs. Releasing his grip on him, Ugly yelped and ran off out the door.

Emily watched in horror as Ugly took off. Poor Ugly. She knew that kick to the ribs was hard enough to hurt him. She only hoped it wasn't too serious of an injury.

"Now, we can do this the hard way, or you can come with me quietly," Mr. Guthrie said. He leaned down and pulling up his pant leg, began rubbing his calf where Ugly had bitten him. Emily could see blood running down his leg from the wound.

"I'm glad Ugly bit you," she said. "You deserve it."

"Well, I think I paid him back pretty good, don't you?" Mr. Guthrie spat out. He looked down at his leg to inspect the wound again.

Thomas took that opportunity and jumped onto Mr. Guthrie's back. He began pummeling him with his fists and yelling. He was no match for Mr. Guthrie, though. Mr. Guthrie reached back and grabbed Thomas by the back of his shirt and yanked him off and threw him to the floor. Thomas landed hard on his back. Stunned, he just laid there looking up at Mr. Guthrie.

"Try that again, kid, and I'll knock you out," Mr. Guthrie said.

Emily watched the goings on and a sudden rage filled her. She was terrified of being taken back with Mr. Guthrie and she was angry that he had hurt Ugly. But when he threw Thomas to the floor, she could no longer hold it in. Flying at him with her arms and legs swinging and kicking, she lit into him with all she had. She managed several hard kicks to his shins and several hits to his stomach and face before he grabbed her around the middle and jerked her up off her feet. He squeezed her so hard she couldn't breathe.

Mercy, who had stood silently off to the side during all of this, let out a roar and jumped at Mr. Guthrie. She screamed the whole time she was hitting and kicking at him.

Thomas jumped to his feet and joined in the assault.

Mr. Guthrie dropped Emily as he tried to fend off the attack.

Once Emily had gotten her breath back, she too, began kicking and hitting him again.

Though he was bigger than any one of them, he couldn't ward off all three of them at once. He turned and ran for the door.

Emily, Thomas and Mercy took chase and followed him out the front door, screaming and yelling at him as they went.

Once they reached the street, Mr. Guthrie stopped and turned around to face them. Dawn was almost upon them and the sky was just beginning to cast light across the horizon. His features were shadowed, but Emily could see the anger and hatred on his face.

"You won't get away with this," he shouted at them. "I'll just bring some of my men back with me."

"Go ahead," shouted Emily. "We won't be here when you get back."

"I'll just find you again," Mr. Guthrie warned.

"No, you won't," said a voice from behind Mr. Guthrie.

Mr. Guthrie swung around just as Emily, Thomas and Mercy saw the sheriff step out from the shadows. Along with him were Sam, Bessie and two deputies.

"Mr. Guthrie, you're under arrest," the sheriff told him.

Mr. Guthrie looked at the sheriff, then turned back to the kids. "These kids belong to me. I'm just here to take back what's rightfully mine, Sheriff."

"These kids told us what's really going on here, Mr. Guthrie," Bessie said.

Mr. Guthrie suddenly turned and started to make a run for it, when Ugly came out of nowhere and jumped on his back, knocking him to the ground. The sheriff sauntered over to where he lay face down in the dirt and pointed his pistol at him. "Taken down by a dog, huh? You aren't the tough guy you pretend to be, are you?"

The two deputies walked over and grabbed Mr. Guthrie by the arms and hauled him to his feet. The sheriff slapped cuffs on him and led him down the street toward the jail.

Bessie ran to the kids and enveloped each one of them in a big hug.

"How did you know Mr. Guthrie was here?" Emily asked her.

"After you told us you saw him in the window, we knew he would come back and try to kidnap you again, so we waited up all night and watched the church from over there behind that stand of trees," Bessie explained, pointing to a spot not far from the church. "When we saw Ugly go into the church, we watched as Mr. Guthrie used that opportunity to get inside too. He just slipped in through the open door. Once he went in, we went and got the sheriff. Shortly after we returned, we heard all the commotion going on inside and were going to go straight in, but then you all came out and we watched as you three kids chased Mr. Guthrie into the street. I must say, it took us all by surprise. I'm so proud of all three of you."

"What's going to happen now?" Thomas asked.

"Let's head down to the jail and see what the sheriff can tell us," Bessie said.

Ugly came limping over to them and whimpered. Emily knelt down and gave him a hug around his neck. "You saved the day, Ugly."

Thomas and Mercy each knelt down in front of Ugly and rubbed his head and gave him a quick hug.

"He's a good dog to have around," Thomas said.

"We's gonna has ta keep 'im fo sho now," Mercy said.

The three kids, Ugly, Bessie and Sam headed for the jail.

The jailhouse was a small, single room with only two cells and a desk for the sheriff. It was dark and dank inside. The single window that was positioned behind the desk, was the only source of outside light.

The sheriff was lighting candles, as the five of them entered. Ugly decided to trot off down the street again, presumably looking for food again.

Mr. Guthrie had been placed into one of the cells and was glaring at them as they crowded around the sheriff's desk.

"So what happens now?" Thomas asked.

"I've sent word off to the surrounding towns to be on the lookout for Mr. Guthrie's men. They'll be hard to find, I'm sure, but it's the best we can do," said the sheriff. "At least we have Mr. Guthrie. If he's the ringleader of the outfit, then we at least put a crimp in their plans."

Mr. Guthrie grumbled something, but no one could make out what he said, so they all ignored him.

"Do you think we'll be safe now," Emily asked.

"I don't know," said the sheriff. "But I'd keep an eye out for the other men if I were you. Until we have them all in custody, I wouldn't consider you completely safe."

"Let's get out of here and get some breakfast," Sam said. He hastily ushered Bessie and the kids out the door and into the street.

"Why did we leave so abruptly?" Thomas asked Sam.

"It's not a good idea to discuss any plans you have in front of Mr. Guthrie. If he gets a chance, he could pass any information he gets on to his men and that could put you three in more danger."

"Oh, I hadn't thought of that," Thomas said. "Thank you."

Sam nodded and led them all down the street to the restaurant. They chose a table at the front of the restaurant next to the big glass window that faced the street.

While they were enjoying their cooked oatmeal and toast, they discussed their upcoming plans.

"Mrs. Thorne usually shows up in town around mid morning," Sam told them. "It takes her several hours to travel this far and she likes to get an early start so she can get her supplies and get home before it gets dark."

"Iffn she's blind, why do it matter iffn she gits home afore dark?" Mercy asked.

"Traveling in these parts after dark isn't safe, especially if you're blind," Bessie said. "There are some bad folks who like to lie in wait along deserted roads for wagons and such to come by so they can rob them. We took a real risk traveling here last night."

A shiver ran up Emily's spine. "I'm glad that didn't happen to us last night, then."

"Yes, me too," Bessie said. "I always carry my pistol with me when I travel, but I'm very glad I didn't have to use it last night."

Emily's jaw dropped open. "You have a gun?"

"Of course," Bessie answered. "It would be foolish to travel anywhere these days without one."

Just as they were finishing up their meal, an old, rickety wagon pulled up alongside the mercantile store across the street. Sam quickly wiped his mouth on his napkin, pushed his seat back and stood up. "That's Mrs. Thorne now," he said. "She's early. I'll just run across the street and have a quick chat with her. You all wait here. I'll come get you once I've talked with her." He hurried out the door and across the street.

"Why couldn't we all go?" Emily asked.

"Mrs. Thorne is a bit eccentric. It's best if Sam talks to her first before you all meet her. I'm sure she'll be happy to take you all with her, but it's best if Sam explains things to her about your situation first."

They all turned in their seats to watch the exchange between Sam and Mrs. Thorne. At first, they stood next to Mrs. Thorne's wagon, with Sam doing the talking. Then all of sudden, Mrs. Thorne snapped her head in the direction of the restaurant as though she could see them through the big window. She hiked up her skirts and grabbed Sam by the arm. She nodded her head toward the restaurant and said something to Sam. He took her hand and laced it through his arm and led her across the street to the restaurant.

As they approached the table, Emily saw that Mrs. Thorne was a tiny, but strong looking woman. She was just under five feet tall and barely weighed eighty pounds. Her silver hair was piled neatly on top of her head and she wore a very plain, drab brown dress, but the tilt of her chin and her ramrod straight back showed signs of a dignity and strength within her.

Sam stopped in front of the table and introduced her to the kids. She turned her head to each one of them when they said hello to her.

"So, there are three of you, huh?" she asked.

"Yes, ma'am," said Emily.

"Well, it's good to meet you," Mrs. Thorne said. "And please call me Nellie. If you're going to be staying with me, I don't see the need in using formalities. I'll be calling you by your given names."

"I explained the situation to Nellie and she has agreed to let you go home with her," Sam said. "She can explain the particulars of things herself."

Thomas, Emily and Mercy all exchanged looks, but didn't say anything.

"I've got plenty of supplies to pick up," Nellie said. "You three can start by helping me load the wagon. Sound good to you?"

"We would be glad to help out," Thomas said.

"Yes, ma'am," Emily said.

"Yes'm," said Mercy. As soon as she had said this, Nellie jerked her head in Mercy's direction.

"Mercy, is it?" She asked. "You don't sound like a white child."

"No ma'am," Mercy said. "I's a colored girl."

"Well, no matter," said Nellie. "I don't care what color you are. If you're willing to help me out, I'd be glad to have you."

"Tank ya, ma'am," Mercy said.

Thomas, Emily and Mercy all said goodbye to Sam and Bessie. Even though they had only known each other for a short time, it was hard to say goodbye. Emily knew she would never forget them, nor all they had done for them.

As Bessie and Sam left the restaurant and headed for Sam's house, Nellie took Thomas by the arm and they walked across the street to the mercantile, followed by Emily and Mercy.

After gathering up all the supplies they would need, such as bags of chicken feed, grain for the horses and Nellie's supply of dried goods, Thomas and the young man running the mercantile in Sam's place, loaded it all into the back of Nellie's wagon.

While the men were busy loading the wagon, Nellie took the girls over to the tailor's shop to get new dresses.

"I just can't see you girls wearing those boy's clothes any longer," Nellie said, shaking her head. "How have you managed it for so long?"

"They're actually quite comfortable," Emily said.

"Well, I ain't having it. Not as long as you're under my roof. Boys will dress like boys and girls will dress like girls."

Emily and Mercy looked at each other and giggled. Nellie probably would have never known that they were dressed like boys if Thomas hadn't said something about it. Nellie had offered to let the girls ride up on the seat of the wagon with her so they didn't act unladylike or get their dresses messed up by riding in the back. Thomas was quick to point out that it wouldn't matter due to the fact that they were wearing pants. Nellie put her foot down and insisted that they were going to go get dresses and no arguments would be allowed.

Emily picked out a soft blue printed dress with fine pinstripes on it, while Mercy picked out a yellow one with white flowers all over it.

After getting final alterations, they slipped the dresses on and turned to each other. Emily had to admit, it was nice to look like a girl again.

She watched Mercy spin around in a circle, looking at herself in the full length mirror. What a truly beautiful girl she was. The yellow of the dress was perfect on her. It gave her dark skin a warm glow and really brought out the deep brown of her eyes. Emily looked at her hair and wondered what could be done with it, though. It was still in it's spiky little braids.

Emily was just about to say something about their hair when the seamstress walked over to them and examined the dresses to make sure they were a perfect fit. "I don't believe I could have done a better job," she said. "You two look beautiful."

"Wha we gonna do 'bout our hair, doe?" Mercy asked before Emily had the chance.

The woman looked at Emily's hair, then at Mercy's. "Well, for you," she indicated to Emily. "I think we should get rid of the updo and brush it out and maybe do a long braid. What do you think?"

Emily nodded and began pulling the pins out of her hair as the woman turned to Mercy. "Oh dear. I don't know much about a colored person's hair, but I think we need to get rid of those braids and maybe just brush it out real good. What do you think?"

Mercy thought about this for a moment, then said, "I kinda like da braids. It gits all fuzzy iffn ya brush it. I tink I'll jus keep my braids."

"Suit yourself," the woman said. "It does actually look rather cute on you." She gave Mercy a warm smile and turned her attention back to Emily.

Emily's hair was loosed from it's pins and the woman began to brush it out. After all the tangles were gone, she tightly braided it and fastened a blue ribbon at the end. Emily examined herself in the mirror. Yes, it was nice to look like a girl again.

Nellie paid for the dresses and they headed outside to find Thomas.

Thomas had gone looking for Ugly, but couldn't find him anywhere. He checked the tavern, the restaurant and anywhere else he could find to look. Just as he was about to give up, he saw Emily, Mercy and Nellie emerge from the tailor's shop. One look at Emily and his heart skipped a beat. She looked so beautiful. He didn't realize such a pretty girl hid beneath those boy's clothes. He gulped and made his way over to them.

"I can't seem to find Ugly," he said, unable to take his eyes off Emily.

"We have to leave," Emily said. "We can't leave him behind."

"Whose Ugly?" Nellie asked.

"He's our dog," Emily said. "He's been with us since we escaped those horrible men."

"Well, we can't wait around much longer to leave," Nellie said. "It's gonna be almost dark by the time we make it my place as it is."

"Let me check the back of the restaurant one more time," Thomas said. "He likes to hang out around places where he can get some food."

Emily and Mercy waited at the wagon with Nellie while Thomas took off for the restaurant.

He walked around to the back and there he found a little girl sitting on the stoop with Ugly curled up on the ground beside her, his head in her lap. He had a bandage wrapped all the way around his middle.

"Ugly, there you are," Thomas scolded him.

Ugly whimpered, but didn't get up.

"Come on, boy, we gotta go."

Ugly thumped his tail on the ground, but still didn't move.

A woman stepped out of the door and onto the stoop. "Young man," she said. "Is this your dog?"

"Yes, ma'am. Well, no ma'am. Well, it's hard to explain. You see, he kind of just follows us around wherever we go, but he isn't really ours."

"Well, he's hurt. I'm guessing someone did something to him," the woman said. "We took him to the doctor and he told us one of his ribs is broken. He patched him up as best he could, but advised us to let him rest so he could heal."

Thomas walked over and knelt down next to the little girl and Ugly. "I'm so sorry, boy," he said, petting his head. "You saved us and we're so thankful to you for that."

He looked up at the woman and down at the little girl. "Will you guys take good care of him?"

"He's my new puppy," the little girl said. "Mama said we can keep him."

"We'll take real good care of him," the mother said. "I promise."

Thomas nodded at her and leaned down and stroked Ugly's head again. "I guess this is goodbye then."

Ugly whimpered and thumped his tail again, but still didn't get up. Thomas knew Ugly had found his new home. With sadness in his heart, he thanked the woman and her daughter and headed back to the wagon.

"Did you find him?" Emily asked.

Thomas explained what had happened and watched as Emily and Mercy cried. He wanted to comfort them, but didn't know how, so he crawled into the back of the wagon and made himself comfortable among all the supplies. It was going to be a long trip to Nellie's place and he was ready to get going.

The girls didn't want to ride up front with Nellie, so with lots of pleading, she finally allowed them to ride in the back with Thomas.

As Emily was climbing into the wagon, she asked Nellie, "How do you know where to go?"

"I don't," Nellie said. "But these horses have made this trip so many times, they could do it blindfolded. I just give them their heads and they take me home every time."

Once the three of them were settled in the back of the wagon, Nellie snapped the reins on the horses backs and the wagon jerked forward and they headed out of town.

CHAPTER 16

The ride up to Nellie's place was slow. The horses plodded along at their own pace and didn't seem to be in much of a hurry. The sun beat down on them and the heat of the day made the ride even more uncomfortable.

Nellie sat in her seat and didn't say a word, while Thomas, Emily and Mercy swayed back and forth in the back as the wagon rolled along the rutted, dirt road.

"I wonder how much longer it'll be till we get there?" Emily asked. They had been traveling for several hours already and there was nothing to be seen on either side of the road except wooded areas and the occasional field. They hadn't seen a homestead or farm since they drove out of the town.

"I don't know, but my backside sure could use a break," said Thomas, adjusting in his seat to try to find a more comfortable position.

"I's kinda likin' dis ride," Mercy said. "It sho is peaceful and quiet. I don like da towns much."

"Well, it is quiet, that's for sure," Thomas said.

Emily turned toward Nellie and called up to her. "Nellie," she said. "How much farther till we get to your place?"

"Oohhhh, we're about half way there by now, I suspect."

"Half way?" Emily asked. "But we've been traveling for hours."

"I know that. But it takes as long as it takes," Nellie answered her. "That's why I start off so early in the morning. The return trip takes a bit longer due to the horses having to pull so much extra weight. They now have you three as added weight as well. Don't worry, though, we'll still reach the home place before dark."

With a deep sigh, Emily settled back down in her seat and got comfortable.

The wagon trundled along for a few more miles, then turned to the right off the road and onto a narrow path. Tree branches hung low over the trail like a canopy. Several of them smacked the sides of the wagon and rained leaves down into the wagon on top of them. The path began a steady ascent and the ground became more rocky the higher they went. The wagon began to bog down and the horses pace slowed to a crawl.

"Whoa," Nellie called to the team. "Kids, I'm going to need you to jump out and walk behind the wagon for a spell, if you don't mind."

"Why?" Emily asked. "What's wrong?"

"The climb up the mountain is going to get steeper and the horses are having a rough time pulling all the extra weight. I'm hoping that with you kids out of the wagon, they will have an easier time of it. They aren't as young as they used to be and this trip gets harder and harder for them each time we go."

Thomas jumped down from the wagon and helped Emily and Mercy to the ground.

"We're out," Thomas called to Nellie.

"Thank you," said Nellie. "You won't have to walk for too long. Once we crest the top of the mountain, you can climb back in again."

Nellie slapped the reins on the horses backs and they jerked forward, pulling the wagon along with them. Even though they moved slowly, they seemed to have an easier time of it.

Thomas, Emily and Mercy trudged along behind the wagon. It wasn't hard to keep up at the pace the horses were going.

"This sure beats sitting in the back of the wagon," Thomas said. "I sure needed to stretch my legs."

"I agree," said Emily.

"We's goin' up hill, doe," Mercy said. "We's gonna git tired real fast."

"I'm ok with that for now," Thomas said. "Nellie said it wasn't too far till we get to the top."

The path was rough. There were several times when the horses had to gain their footing in order to keep the wagon from going backward. Loose rocks and deep ruts made the trail hard to navigate at times, but the horses pulled through and eventually, the path smoothed out enough to make traveling on it more manageable.

They walked for over an hour when the ground began to level out beneath their feet.

Emily realized just how hard it must be for the horses since she, herself, was panting and sweat was rolling down her back with the effort of climbing the steep mountainside.

When the wagon leveled off at the top of the trail, Nellie pulled back on the reins stopping the horses. "Time for a short break," she said to the kids.

Thomas was almost out of breath and flopped down to the ground and lay on his back looking up at the sky. Emily dropped down next to him and let out a long sigh. Mercy stopped where she had stood and looked around her in all directions.

"Em, Tom," she said. "Git back up here and come look at dis."

"I'm too tired to move right now," Thomas said. "What is it?"

Emily looked up at Mercy from the ground and was curious about the look on her face. She was standing there with her mouth wide open and her eyes about to pop out of her head. She was slowly turning her head in all directions, looking at something that Emily couldn't see. Curiosity got the better of her and she got up and stood beside Mercy.

"Look at dat, Em," Mercy said, pointing ahead of her.

Emily looked to where Mercy was pointing and gasped. The view from the mountaintop was breathtaking. Through the trees, she could see mountain ranges that stretched for miles and miles. Blue, hazy clouds seemed to cling to the tops and drift down into the valleys below. The sun was starting it's descent from the sky and it's rays were casting beautiful shadows across the tree covered slopes.

Emily didn't think she had ever seen anything more beautiful. She slowly swiveled her head in every direction taking in the beauty of her surroundings.

"It's gorgeous, isn't it?" Nellie asked.

Curious now, Thomas jumped to his feet and joined the girls. He scanned the horizon, but couldn't find the words to describe how truly beautiful it was.

"You've seen it before?" Emily asked.

"Of course," Nellie said. "I wasn't always blind, you know. When my husband and I first moved up on this mountain, I could see just as clearly as you can. Old age has robbed me of my eyesight, but my mind still remembers actually what it looks like."

Emily felt a stab of sorrow for Nellie. It seemed a shame to live in such a beautiful place and not be able to see it.

"Come on now," Nellie said. "Let's get going. We still have a ways to go and it'll be getting dark soon."

The three of them crawled back up into the wagon and took their seats behind Nellie. They couldn't take their eyes off the scenery though. Every step they took offered new views and picturesque scenery.

The trail had opened back up to a wider road and they traveled on for several more miles when the horses seemed to quicken their pace. Emily turned around to see what had caused them to speed up.

Just a short ways up ahead a small farm came into view. A little cabin sat in the middle of a large clearing. A barn sat off to the left of the cabin and a garden ran along the side the cabin on the right. The farm was perched atop a small rise and the views from it's location were stunning. It gave Emily the notion of being in the clouds.

Again, the neighboring mountaintops were visible as far as the eye could see. Clouds lay on them like blankets. The sun was almost set, which caused the mountains to be ablaze in orange and red hues. Emily just stared, in a loss for words at the sight before her. Never before had she seen such a beautiful place.

"Ok, kids," Nellie said. "You'll have plenty of time tomorrow to admire the view. Right now, we got work to do."

"What do you call this place?" Thomas asked.

"Heaven's Mountain, is what my husband used to call it. I just simply call it Heaven."

"Heaven," Mercy said. "Dat's fittin'."

"Come on now," Nellie said. "Help me get this wagon unloaded. Tom, if you'll take the grain and feed out to the barn, the girls can help me get the dry goods inside."

Emily grabbed a sack of dry goods and hoisted it over her shoulder. Stepping into the cabin, she looked around. It was small, but plenty big enough for the four of them. The living room had a large fireplace that was centered in the room against the wall. A small kitchen was off to the right and a bedroom was tucked behind the fireplace off of the living room. A ladder went up to a loft where Emily assumed she, Mercy and Thomas would sleep.

The cabin was very tidy and clean. No dust crowded in the corners or along the window panes. No dirt littered the floor. Emily was amazed at how spotless it was. How did Nellie keep it so clean if she couldn't even see it?

Mercy pushed her way through the door and laid her burden of supplies on the floor next to the door.

"Dis be nice," she said to Emily. "I's never lived in such a nice place afore."

Nellie entered the cabin and bustled around the kitchen for a moment, moving saucers and pans out of the way to make room for the new supplies.

"I put Tom to work brushing the horses and getting them in their stalls for the night. You girls can help me put all these supplies away."

At the end of the kitchen, Nellie pulled aside a curtain to reveal a wall full of shelves. Cans and dried goods lined the shelves along with several tubs and canisters filled with things Emily could only guess at.

Nellie explained how everything was arranged so she would be able to find what she needed. She explained that since she couldn't see what something was, it was important to have it all in certain places so she knew where each item was.

Emily and Mercy listened carefully to Nellie's instructions and carefully placed the items exactly where she told them to put them.

Once they had successfully stashed all the supplies away, Nellie went to the fireplace and fiddled around with the logs and stuck a spoon into a pot she had hanging over the coals. "I need one of you to light the fire for me," she said. "I put some stew in the pot to heat up once I got home. I wasn't expecting to feed three extra mouths, but I think there is enough in there to feed us all."

Mercy quickly set to work starting a fire, while Emily helped Nellie lay out plates and cups.

Thomas came in just as the stew was beginning to boil. The savory aroma filled the cabin.

They each filled a plate and took a seat on the floor around the fire.

"While we enjoy our meal," Nellie began. "I want to go over some rules and set down the do's and don'ts of the place. I'll go over the jobs I'll need your help with and we can figure out who will do what."

"We will be glad to help with whatever you need," Emily said. "We're just so thankful you're letting us stay here for awhile."

"Well, it'll be turning to winter in a few short weeks and it gets pretty rough up here in the mountains once the snow starts to fall. You're doing me a huge favor by being here, so I'm thankful to the three of you for agreeing to come along."

"I's not afeared of hard work," Mercy said. "I's used ta it."

"That's a good thing, Mercy," Nellie said. "Cause around here, there's nothing but hard work to be had."

"What happened to your husband?" Thomas asked. "How long have you been alone up here?"

"My Frank died of the fever about two years back now. I've been making do ever since. It hasn't been easy though. I've thought many times of leaving this old mountain and taking up residence in the town, but I just can't seem to leave this place. My heart is here. Frank is buried just up on the rise behind the barn. I visit him every day."

"I'm so sorry, Nellie," Emily said. "You must miss him very badly."

"I sure do, but the good Lord gave us almost fifty years together. I'm just grateful I had him for that long."

They all sat in silence for a while as they ate their food, then Nellie got back down to business. "Alright then, let's see," she said. "Tom, you don't mind if I call you Tom, do you?"

"Not at all. I actually kind of like it better than Thomas."

"Ok then, Tom," Nellie said. "You'll be in charge of the barn and the care of the animals. You ever tend to animals before?"

"No, ma'am, but I figure I can learn pretty quick."

"There ain't much to it, truth be told. Just brush them down when they need it, make sure they have plenty of hay and water and clean out their hooves every once in awhile. That's about it. All I have left now are the horses. I couldn't tend to the sheep and goats anymore due to my lack of eyesight, so I sold them off in town one summer and that left me with just the horses and a few chickens."

"Chickens?" Thomas asked. "What am I supposed to do with them?"

Emily couldn't help but laugh. The look on Tom's face showed that he wasn't real thrilled with the idea of tending to chickens.

"Well, you throw them some grain in the morning and gather up their eggs while they're eating and that's all there is to that. The coop is on this side of the barn. Can't miss it."

"Ok, I can handle that," Thomas said. He was rubbing his hands together and Emily could tell he was anxious about the chickens. She wondered why he was nervous about them.

"You girls will help me with the house keeping, laundry, cooking and cleanup," Nellie told Emily and Mercy.

"I's able to help Tom wif da chickens iffn dat would be ok," Mercy said. She too, had noticed Tom's apprehension and wanted to help him out.

"That's fine, if you want to," Nellie said. "Now, there are some rules we need to go over too. Rule number one, no going outside by yourself at night unless it's to the barn and back. Wild animals roam these parts and I don't want any of you getting attacked. If you have to go outside, take someone with you. Second rule, no cussing or using foul language in my house. I don't abide by that. Third rule, we respect each other. We all have to live together, so let's all try to get along as best we can. Rule number four, do what I tell you. I know what's best about living way up here and if I tell you to do something, or not to do something, there's a good reason for it. Any questions?"

"No, ma'am," the three of them said in unison.

"Alrighty then," Nellie said. "I think we'll all get along just fine."

They finished eating their meal and Emily and Mercy helped Nellie clean up the dishes.

Thomas sat by the fireplace, stoking the coals to keep them lit. He looked around for more firewood, but didn't see any.

"Nellie," he said. "Where's the firewood? I'll go bring some more in to keep the fire going."

"It's out beside the barn. It would be great if you brought in enough to have for in the morning too."

Thomas headed out the door and turned toward the barn. It was dark now and seeing his way over to it was difficult. He stumbled his way around, but eventually found the stack of firewood leaning up against the side of the barn facing the cabin. Loading his arms with several logs, he made his way back to the house. He had to make several trips to get enough to stack beside the fireplace.

"You'll need to add cutting firewood to your list of chores," Nellie said. "We won't have enough to make it through the winter if you don't."

"No problem. I used to cut firewood at the orphanage, so I know how to do that."

When it came time for bed, Nellie pulled out several blankets from an old chest she had in her bedroom. "I don't know how you three are used to sleeping, but in my house, boys and girls who aren't married, do not sleep in the same room. Therefore, Emily and Mercy will take the loft and Tom, you will be on the divan in the living room."

Tom didn't seem too happy about this arrangement, but by the tone of Nellie's voice, there wasn't room for negotiations. He took a blanket from her outstretched arms and walked over to the divan. Emily and Mercy took the other blankets from her and headed up the ladder to the loft. Nellie disappeared behind the curtain that separated her bedroom from the living room.

Once up in the loft, the girls spread the blankets on the floor and prepared for bed. Emily could hear Tom rustling around down below and crept over to the edge of the loft and looked down at him. He was removing his boots and was just about to slip under the blanket when he caught sight of her.

"What are you doing?" he asked in a loud whisper.

"It's just weird, isn't it?" she asked him, whispering back so Nellie wouldn't hear her. "We're all used to sleeping together, so it feels weird with you down there all by yourself."

"It'll be alright, Emily," he said. "Just have to get used to sleeping alone is all."

He slid under the blanket and looked up at her. "Good night, Em."

"Good night, Tom," she said.

Emily crawled back over next to Mercy and laid down. She was surprised to find that Mercy was already asleep.

CHAPTER 17

It was still dark when Nellie woke them up. She was bustling about the kitchen when Emily and Mercy climbed down the ladder.

"Mercy, I need you to go gather us up some eggs for breakfast," Nellie said. "Thomas is out feeding the horses and chickens. Emily, you can help me roll out biscuits."

"It's still dark out dere, Nellie," Mercy said. "How's I gonna see ta git da eggs?"

"Oh my, I didn't realize the sun wasn't up yet. I can't tell anymore," Nellie laughed out loud. "I guess you get to help with the biscuits till the sun rises."

Emily and Mercy watched as Nellie showed them how to mix up the biscuit mix and roll them out. Emily was totally amazed at how well Nellie was able to do everything without being able to see. She watched in fascination as Nellie rolled and cut the biscuits and laid them in a pan. "Nellie," she asked. "How do you do everything without being able to see?"

"Years of doing the same thing. I used to always joke that I could do my chores with my eyes closed since I did them everyday. Now, I guess, I really can."

Emily and Mercy took over rolling and cutting the biscuits and laying them in the pan, while Nellie excused herself and took off for her bedroom.

Once the pan was full, Mercy slid the pan into the oven that Nellie had already lit a fire in. Shutting the door, she turned to Emily. "Wha ya s'pose she doin' in dere? I hope she's not gittin' sick. She took off in a awful big hurry."

"She didn't look sick to me," Emily said. "Maybe she just wanted to get a bit more sleep. She did wake us up really early."

Thomas opened the door to the cabin and stepped inside, slipping his boots off by the door. "Sun's starting to come up," he told the girls.

"I gits ta go git da eggs now," Mercy said excitedly.

"I don't know why you're so excited about that," Tom said. "They can be mean little things."

"I loves chickens," Mercy said. "I use ta help my mama wif dem at da farm we worked at. Dey's sum funny birds."

"Well, you are more than welcome to collect the eggs then," Tom said.

"Why are you so afraid of chickens, Tom?" Emily asked.

"At the orphanage, I was out gathering the eggs one morning and a couple of those stupid birds lit into me. They pecked and kicked me and wouldn't stop till I left the pen. I never went back in. I let another boy named Robert do it after that. I had welts and cuts all over my hands and arms."

Mercy laughed so hard she had to clutch her stomach. "Ya gotta show dem whose boss. Udderwise dey gonna git ya ever' time."

"Yeah well, you are more than welcome to them," Tom said. He couldn't help laughing along with Emily and Mercy.

Nellie finally came out of her bedroom carrying a bundle in her arms. "I've got something for you kids here," she said. She laid the bundle down on the kitchen table. "I dug out a bunch of my old dresses and some of Frank's old clothes. I figure we can alter them to fit you, then you'll have more than just one outfit to wear."

Emily and Mercy began digging through the pile looking at the different dresses and picking which ones they each liked.

"Girls, let's set them aside till after we eat," Nellie suggested. "Mercy, I do believe I heard Tom say the sun is coming up. Those eggs won't gather themselves."

"Yes'm," Mercy said and headed out the door.

Emily set the table and checked on the biscuits, they still had some time to cook before they were done, so she sat down at the table with Nellie. Tom decided to go out and watch Mercy, which amused Emily. He was too afraid to do the job himself, but he had no problem watching Mercy do it. She laughed to her thinking about it.

"Emily," Nellie said. "You've got some good friends there."

"Oh, we're not friends, we're family," Emily told her.

"You have a heart as big as these mountains, you do," Nellie said.

Tom and Mercy came back with several eggs. Nellie instructed the girls how to scramble them over the fire.

Once the biscuits and eggs were done, they sat down at the table to eat.

Nellie seemed to pick at her food and scoot it around on her plate, but didn't eat much of it.

"Nellie, are you ok?" Emily asked her.

"Oh yes, I'm just tired. I think the trip wore me out and I didn't seem to sleep real good last night."

"Why don't you go lay down and we can clean up the breakfast mess," Thomas suggested.

"No, we've got too much to do today," Nellie said. "I want to get those dresses fitted today and have you try on Frank's old clothes to see if they fit. Maybe after we get that done, I'll take a little nap."

Emily and Mercy cleaned up the breakfast dishes and put everything away while Tom took the clothes and stepped behind the curtain into Nellie's bedroom to try them on. By the time the kitchen was cleaned up, Tom found several items that fit him. He brought the rest out and laid them on the table.

"I found several things that fit," he told Nellie. She still seemed very distracted, but she nodded and told the girls to go try on the dresses.

Emily and Mercy tried on several dresses and found they fit perfectly and didn't need any alterations. Nellie was so small that her clothes where more child sized than adult sized anyway.

"You kids can keep any of the clothes that you want to. I don't wear them anymore and you need them more than I do," she told them.

"Thank you very much," Tom said.

"Yes, thank you," said Emily.

"I's never had so many clothes afore. Tank ya, Nellie," Mercy said.

"You are all very welcome," Nellie said. "Now, before I lay down for a nap, I must go see Frank. Would you all like to walk up with me?"

They all agreed to go with her, so they put their boots on and headed out the door.

The sun was high in the sky and a gentle breeze blew across the mountaintop as they followed Nellie up the small rise behind the barn. Emily noticed that it was cooler up here in the mountains than it had been down in the town. The breeze felt good, but there was a slight chill to the air.

At the top of the rise, under a tall, shady tree was a single tombstone. It was made out of a misshapen, thin rock, but the etching in it was clear. It read, *Frank Thorne, Beloved Husband*.

Nellie knelt down on the ground next to the stone and ran her hand across the words. Emily thought she saw a tiny tear slide down her cheek.

Nellie bowed her head and seemed to be talking to herself for a moment, when Emily realized she was saying a prayer. She elbowed Mercy and signaled for Tom to bow his head too. The three of them stood quietly while Nellie offered up her prayer.

After a couple of minutes, Nellie lifted her head and sat down on the ground, her hand still on the grave marker. "Would the three of you please give me a moment alone with him?"

"Of course," Tom said. He grabbed Emily's and Mercy's hands and led them back down the hill to the cabin.

"Oh, I feel so bad for her," Emily said. "She seemed so sad."

"I know," Tom said. "I can't imagine how much she must be missing him."

"She ain't actin' right dis mornin'," Mercy said. "I fink sumpin is wrong wif her."

"What do you mean?" Emily asked.

"She jus actin' diff'ernt is all."

"Well, we really don't know her well enough to know what is normal for her and what isn't," Tom said.

"I know dat, but her's actin' like her ain't feelin' good."

"She's just tired from the trip like she said," Emily said, brushing off Mercy's concern. "She just needs to rest up when she comes back down."

"I's tellin' ya, sumpin is wrong wif 'er."

"Let's go back up and check on her," Tom said. "Mercy's making me nervous."

They climbed back up the hill. Nellie was laying on the ground next to the grave. She seemed to be sleeping, but she was crumpled up in an odd position. Tom ran to her, followed closely by Emily and Mercy.

When Tom reached her, he dropped down on his knees next to her and shook her shoulder. "Nelllie? Nellie, wake up."

"What's wrong with her, Tom?" Emily asked shakily. "Why isn't she moving."

Tom leaned down and put his ear to her mouth. No breath came out. No sound was heard at all. He shook her harder and called out louder. "Nellie! Nellie, wake up."

All the blood had drained out of his face as he turned to the girls. He was visibly shaking and couldn't seem to find his words.

"Tom, what's wrong," Emily yelled at him. "Wake her up, Tom! Wake her up!"

"I can't," he said. "I think she's dead."

Mercy let out a gasp and turned her back to them. "I tole ya sumpin was wrong. I tole ya."

"What are we going to do?" Emily asked. She had never been so scared in her life. What were they supposed to do now? What were they going to do with Nellie?

"I don't know," Tom said. He was in a daze and couldn't seem to wrap his head around what had just happened.

"We's got ta bury her," Mercy said, turning back to face them. "We can't jus leaves her layin' dere."

"We need to go get help," Emily said.

"Where are we going to get help from?" Tom demanded. "We're miles from anywhere. It would take us hours to get back to town."

"Well, we have to do something," Emily shouted.

"We's got ta bury her," Mercy said. She was oddly calm. Emily looked at her and was stunned to see that she didn't have any emotion on her face.

"We can't just bury her, Mercy. What's wrong with you?"

"I's seen deaf afore. Dere's nuffin we can do fo her now. We's got ta bury her next ta her husband."

Tom looked at Mercy and slowly nodded his head. "Mercy's right. There's nothing we can do. She's dead. Even if we go get help, there's nothing anyone can do. We have to bury her."

Emily began to cry in earnest. Her whole body was wracked with sobs. "Why did this happen? Poor Nellie."

"Her's at peace now. Her's wif her husband agin. I know she'd be happy 'bout dat," Mercy said. She walked over and knelt down next to Nellie's lifeless body. "It's ok, now Nellie," she said, softly. "We's gonna put ya next ta yo husband where ya belongs."

Tom stood there staring at Mercy. He was dumbfounded at how calm she was. "Are you ok, Mercy?" he asked. "How come you're not upset?"

"Deaf isn' a bad ting. It's jus sumpin dat happens to ever'one eventually. My mama seys deaf takes us ta da next place which is much bedder den dis one. So I know dat Nellie is in a bedder place."

Tom and Emily just stared at her. Mercy ignored them and began straightening out Nellie's rumpled clothing. "Tom, we's gonna need a shovel. Em, see iffn ya can find Nellie's Bible in da house and bring it up here. I's gonna see iffn I can find a rock or sumpin ta use as a head stone."

Tom and Emily continued to just stare at her. She looked up from attending Nellie and said, "Now!"

Tom and Emily both sprang into action and ran back down the hill to the cabin.

Tom ran into the barn and began looking around for a shovel, while Emily searched Nellie's bedroom for her Bible. She found it tucked under her pillow. Grabbing it, she ran back out to the barn to find Tom.

Together they headed back up the hill with the shovel and Bible. When they reached the grave site, they found Mercy cleaning off a rock she had found. "I don know how ta carve her name in dis, but we can put it here to mark her grave anyway."

"Thanks, Mercy," Tom said. "That's a nice rock you found. It'll work great."

Tom set to work digging a hole next to Nellie's husband's grave. Emily sat on the ground a few feet away and watched, stunned. She still couldn't believe that Nellie was gone. She had just been sitting at the kitchen table with her talking not more than an hour ago.

Mercy was using the hem of her dress to clean the rock off. She still seemed oddly calm to Emily. How many people had Mercy seen die that she would be so calm? The thought left Emily uneasy. It was hard enough to see Nellie dead. They barely knew her, but what if it had been one of them? A shiver ran up her spine and a wave of nausea washed over her. She swallowed hard and squeezed her eyes shut. She didn't want to watch anymore.

It took Tom a long time to dig a hole deep enough to put Nellie's body into. Emily didn't offer to help. She was scared and the thought of digging a grave was bound to give her nightmares.

Mercy had finished cleaning the rock and had set it next to Nellie's body. She sat down next to Emily and put her arm around her. "It's gonna be ok, Em," she said. "We's gonna be ok."

"How do you know that, Mercy?"

"We was ok da whole time we was alone in da woods t'gedder. We's gonna be ok now too. We can stay in da cabin and we has pleny of food now."

Emily thought about what Mercy had just told her. It was true. They managed to survive in the woods once they escaped the men and now, at least, they had the cabin to stay in and plenty of food t eat.

Tom threw the shovel down and wiped his sweaty, dirty arm across his forehead leaving a muddy streak. "I think it's deep enough now."

"What do we do now?" Emily asked.

"We have to put her in it," Tom said.

A whole new horror filled Emily. She had to touch Nellie? She had to help put her in the grave?

"Oh no, no, no," she cried. "I can not touch her!"

"Emily, you have to help," Tom said. "Mercy and I can't do it on our own. We all have to help."

Her eyes wide with fear and panic, she looked to Mercy for help.

"Tom's right, we's gotta do it t'gedder."

Emily felt fear seize up her whole body. "I can't," she barely breathed out.

"Oh yes ya can," Mercy scolded her. "Git a grip on yoself. You's gotta help us."

Emily stood up and wrung her hands. Sweat was rolling down her back and she could hardly breathe. She started to step away from them, when Tom came up behind her and threw his arms around her, holding her tightly to himself. "It's ok, Em. It'll all be over with soon. Just help us roll her into the grave and I'll do the rest."

She clung to him desperately, tears running down her face. Slowly a strength she didn't realize she had began to build in her. She could do this. She had to do this. She had to help her friends, her family. They needed her.

She pushed herself out of Tom's arm and slowly nodded, wiping her eyes with the backs of her hands. "Ok," she said, barely above a whisper. "I'll help."

"Ok, you and Mercy get on this side of her and I'll get on the other side. I'll pull while you two push," Tom said.

Once they were all in position, Tom grabbed Nellie's arm and the side of her skirt and began to pull while Emily and Mercy pushed from their side. Little by little, they managed to get her over to the side of the hole. Tom joined them on the side they were on and together they rolled her into her grave. She landed with a thud on her back. The three of them just stared down at her for a moment before Tom grabbed the shovel and began pitching dirt down on top of her.

Once the hole was filled in and the rock was set in place, Tom picked up the Bible and opened it to Psalms 23 and began to read. Emily and Mercy bowed their heads in silence.

When he finished, they turned and headed back down the hill to the cabin, each lost in his or her own thoughts.

CHAPTER 18

The next couple of weeks passed in a blur for Emily. The three of them stayed busy learning all the things they would have to do to survive on their own in the little cabin atop the mountain.

Tom had tried and failed many times to harness the horses up to the wagon, but was unable to do so. He had never had to do anything like it at the orphanage and all the different straps and belts and buckles confused him. He finally gave up.

Mercy was great at tending to the chickens. She loved chasing them around the yard and whenever one of them tried to peck at her, she fended it off without getting herself hurt. Tom marveled at how at ease she was with them. She also proved to be a very good cook. She enjoyed spending time in the kitchen and her creations delighted Tom and Emily. She tended the garden and brought in the fresh vegetables whenever they needed picked.

Emily realized that her life of luxury living in the big mansion with her father and being catered to by Olive had left her with little skills. She had blisters on her hands from scrubbing the laundry and she had burned herself numerous times trying to help Mercy with the cooking. She did discover, though, that she was good at keeping the cabin clean and organized.

Once each of them had figured out what they were good at, those became the daily chores they were each responsible for. Life on the farm was hard, but they learned as they went and helped each other when they could.

The sun seemed dim this morning as Emily opened the front door to sweep the dust out. She squinted her eyes as she took in the sweeping views. There was a definite chill to the air and the color of the leaves was beginning to change. She heard Tom out in the barn cleaning the stalls and Mercy was humming to herself as she picked the vegetables from the garden that she would need for dinner. Emily smiled to herself. They really were a family.

Tom stepped out of the barn and stomped his feet a few times. Seeing Emily standing at the door, he lifted his arm and waved. Emily's heart skipped a beat. She waved back at him and felt a warm flush spread across her cheeks. She watched as he stepped back into the barn and disappeared.

Mercy, with her hands full of vegetables, began to giggle.

"What are you laughing at?" Emily asked her.

"I tink ya has a crush on 'im," Mercy said, inclining her head toward the barn.

"Nah uh," Emily said. "You don't know what you're talking about."

"Mmhmm."

"I do not have a crush on Tom," Emily said. "He's our brother."

"Mebbe by choice, but not by blood," Mercy said. "I don see nuffin wrong wif ya likin' 'im."

"Ooh hush now. He'll hear you."

"So, it's true?" Mercy giggled again.

"I didn't say that."

"Ya don haf ta. I sees it on yo face ever' time ya looks at 'im."

Emily turned on her heel and walked back inside. Mercy followed and dropped the vegetables on the table.

"What are we having for dinner today?" Emily asked, changing the topic.

"We's runnin' low on stuff. I jus pulled da las of da veggies outta da garden. So I's tinking we's jus gonna have da veggies and a bit of da bread I made yes'aday."

"We need more food if we're going to make it through the winter. We need to make a trip to town."

"Dat's a long ways. How's we gonna pay fo da food even if we does go?"

"Hhmmm, I hadn't thought of that."

"Wha did Nellie use when she went?" Mercy asked.

"I don't know. She must have had money."

"Well, when yous cleanin' da place, did ya fine any money anywheres?"

"No, but I hadn't really been looking for any. I've just been cleaning, not searching for anything."

"Well, I guess ya need ta start searchin' while I's makin' dinner."

Emily nodded and began searching the living room area. Tom was still sleeping on the couch at night since none of them felt right about taking Nellie's bed. They had closed the curtain after she died and had not gone back there since. Emily eyed the curtain, but didn't make a move toward it. Instead, she searched the kitchen, the loft and the living room again, but found nothing.

"Yous gonna haf ta go back dere ya know," Mercy told her. She was cutting up the vegetables and never lifted her eyes from her chore as she spoke.

"I was hoping I didn't have to, but I guess you're right. Would you come with me please?"

"No, I's gettin' dinner ready. I's right here doe, so yous gonna be jus fine. Iffn ya need me, den call me."

"I need you. I'm calling you now."

"Oh for Pete's sake, Em."

"Come on, please?"

"Fine. But let's hurry up. I's gettin' hungry."

Emily gingerly pulled back the curtain to Nellie's room and paused. She glanced around the room, but didn't go in.

"Wha's ya waitin' fo? Git in dere," Mercy said, shoving her from behind.

Emily let out a squeal as she was pushed into the room. "Mercy!"

"Well, I tole ya...I was in a hurry."

"Ugh, fine," Emily said. "Help me look."

The girls scoured the room, but didn't find any money anywhere. They had searched the chest, the small dresser, under the bed, under the mattress and on the small night stand beside the bed. Emily let out a long sigh and plopped down on the bed.

"Nothing," she said.

"Well, we tried," Mercy said. "Guess we'll haf ta fine 'nother way ta pay fo da food."

Neither of the girls heard Tom enter the house. He threw back the curtain and stepped into the small room. Emily screamed and jumped up from the bed. Mercy spun around and almost clobbered him.

"Whoa," Tom said, warding off a blow from Mercy. "What are you two doing?"

"We were looking for money," Emily said. "We're almost out of food and we need to make a trip to town before winter hits."

"Well, we're in luck," Tom said, pulling a jar out from behind his back where he had it hidden. "Look what I found in the barn."

Emily grabbed the jar and examined it's contents. It was full of money. She unscrewed the lid and dumped it out onto the bed. "Quick, let's count it," she said and she began sorting the dollar bills from the coins.

"Yous guys can count it," Mercy said. "I's gonna go finish up makin' dinner." She turned to leave, but not before she caught Emily's eye and winked at her, nodding her head toward Tom.

Emily rolled her eyes and went back to sorting the money.

"What's with the eye rolling?" Tom asked.

Emily's head snapped up and she looked at him with her mouth open. "Uh...nothing," she said.

"Are you mad that she wanted to go finish dinner?"

"No, not at all."

"Then why the eye rolls, Em?" Tom pressed.

"Ugh, if you must know, Mercy thinks I have a crush on you, alright?" Emily laughed trying to make a joke of it, but Tom just stared at her.

"Do you?" he asked her, not laughing at all.

"No, of course not," Emily said, trying to make herself believe it.

Tom just looked curiously at her for several moments, then went back to counting the money.

"Well, it looks like we have more than enough to get food and supplies," he said. "I just need to learn how to harness up those horses so we can make the trip to town."

"You'd better learn quick. Did you feel how cold the air is getting in the early morning and evenings?"

"Yeah, I did," Tom said. "I'm guessing it's around September or maybe even October by now."

"Nellie said it got cold sooner up here in the mountains than it does down in town. Do you think it's going to snow soon?" Emily asked.

"I think it's possible," Tom said. He kept looking at her in ways that made her stomach feel weird.

"Why do you keep looking at me like that?" she asked him.

"No reason," he answered. "Let's go tell Mercy how much money we found. She'll be happy to know we can afford food."

He quickly turned from her and slipped out of the room.

Emily sat on the edge of the bed for several moments, thinking of what she had told Tom. Did she have a crush on him? *No, that's ridiculous*, she told herself. Though she had to admit, he was rather attractive. She had started to notice little things about him that she hadn't previously taken any notice of. Like how dark his hair really was. It was so dark, it was almost black. She had noticed the other night at dinner that his eyes were green with brown flecks in them. She liked how tall he was and noticed that he was strong and rather muscular. "Oh my," she said to herself. "I think I *do* have a crush on him." She shook the thought from her head and went out to join him and Mercy in the kitchen.

They had just finished cleaning up the dinner dishes when a knock sounded at the door. They all jumped in their seats, but none of them made a move toward the door.

"Who is that? Who would be knocking on the door?" Emily asked, fear lacing her words.

"Don open da door. We don know who's out dere," Mercy said, whispering.

The knock sounded at the door again and a male voice called out, "Hello Nellie. It's me, Jack."

"Whose Jack?" Tom mouthed to the girls.

"Nellie? You in there?"

"I'm going to answer the door," Tom said, getting up from his seat.

"No, Tom!" Emily cried.

"Sshhh, it's ok," Tom said.

He walked over to the door and called through it. "Nellie's not here right now."

"Oh," came the reply. "Who are you?"

Tom pulled the door slowly open and stuck his head out. "I'm Tom. I'm staying here with Nellie," he said.

"Well, hello Tom," said the man on the other side of the door. "I'm Jack. I'm a good friend of Nellie's. I always stop in to check on her on my way through this area."

Tom swung the door open and stepped back letting the man in. He was an older man close to Nellie's age. He had a long, gray beard and hair that reached almost to his waist. Flung over his shoulder was a rifle.

"Hello, Jack," Tom said. He nodded toward the girls. "This is Emily and Mercy."

"Howdy girls," Jack said. He slid the rifle off his shoulder and propped it against the wall behind the door. "You got anymore grub I could eat?"

Mercy quickly set out a plate and laid some of the bread and vegetables on it and set it down on the table. Jack pulled up a seat and began eating. He seemed oblivious to the three sets of eyes on him.

When he finished, he shoved the plate back and rubbed his stomach. "I thank you for that," he said, directing his gratitude toward Mercy.

"Yous welcome," she said.

"Now," Jack said. "Where's Nellie?"

The kids all pulled up a chair at the table and sat down. Tom looked at the girls and shrugged. Emily nodded at him, but didn't say a word.

"Come on now," Jack said. "Out with it."

Tom cleared his throat and said, "She passed, sir. About two weeks ago now."

"Well, I'll be," Jack said. "I wondered how much longer she could hold on, what with her bad heart and all."

"She had a bad heart?" Emily asked.

"Sure did," Jack said. "It's a wonder she lived as long as she did. When her Frank died, I thought she'd go with him, but she hung on here for two years. Bless her soul. I'm gonna miss her."

"You said you stop by on your way through," Tom said. "Where are you headed?"

"I live on the next mountain over. I'm coming back from my run to town. I always stop in here on my way through to check on her. Make sure she's getting along ok."

"We needs ta make a trip ta town ourselves soon," Mercy said.

Jack eyed her for a minute, then said, "How did you manage to be here?"

"Nellie brung me up here ta help her out fo da winter, same as Tom and Emily here," Mercy said.

"Huh, well, that was kind of her," Jack replied. "You being a blackie and all, I was just surprised to see you is all."

"Is there a problem with that?" Tom asked, an edge of anger in his voice. He reached under the table and grabbed Mercy's hand.

"No, none at all as far as I'm concerned," said Jack. "Just was a tad surprised is all."

"She's one of us now," Emily said. "We don't call her a blackie. She's our family."

"I'm truly sorry, young lady. I meant no offense," Jack said. He looked at each one of the kids in turn. "You kids staying here all alone then?"

"Yes, sir," said Tom. "We plan on spending the winter here, at least."

"You know how to handle yourselves ok, then?"

"What do you mean?" Tom asked.

"The winter can bring some dangers around these parts. You have to know how to take care of yourselves," Jack said. "You ever shoot a gun, son?"

"N..no, sir," Tom stammered.

"Well, now. Every young man ought to know how to shoot a gun to protect his women folk. Tell you what," Jack said. "Tomorrow, I'll take you out and show you how and you can practice till you learn the right proper way to use one. What do you say?"

"You're staying the night here?" Emily asked.

"I always do," Jack said. "Nellie let's me bunk in the barn."

"Ya can stay in Nellie's room, iffn ya want ta," Mercy said. "We don sleep in dere."

Jack looked from Mercy to Tom. "Is that alright with you?"

"Sure," Tom said. "It sure beats the barn."

Jack nodded. "Thank you, then. I sure wouldn't mind a comfy bed for a night."

"Sir," Tom began. "Do you know how to hitch up the horses to the wagon?"

"Yup, sure do."

"Could you teach me?"

"Looks like I may need to stay for a few days. Seems I might have quite a lot of things to teach you."

Tom looked at Emily and Mercy and raised his eyebrows as if to ask if it was ok. Emily and Mercy both smiled and nodded. "It's ok with me," Emily said.

"I's ok wif it," Mercy said.

It was starting to get dark, so Jack took his horse out to the barn and stabled him in one of the empty stalls. He pulled his small wagon into the barn and left it there as well.

Emily had gone back into Nellie's room and gathered up all the money and stuffed it back into the jar and carried it up to the loft. She didn't know yet whether or not Jack could be trusted, but wasn't taking any chances.

The evening wore on with them sitting around the fireplace as Jack told them stories of mountain living. Jack had been born and raised on the next mountain over and didn't know any other kind of life style. Emily was in awe of him as he told of fighting off mountain lions, shooting himself a black bear and making a rug out of its hide and of snow storms so bad, he couldn't leave his house for days.

"Sir," Emily asked. "How old are you?"

Jack scratched his beard and drew his eyebrows together in a questioning manner. "I don't rightly know," he said. "I never really counted."

"You don't know how old you are?" Tom asked.

"No, I guess I don't," Jack said. "It never really mattered. How old are you young'uns?"

"I'm fifteen," Tom said.

"I'm thirteen," said Emily. "I'll be fourteen in October."

"I's tirteen too," said Mercy. "I's gonna be fourteen in October too."

Emily was shocked to hear this. "I didn't know your birthday was in October too."

"Ya never asked," Mercy said.

"You'll be happy to know that October will be here soon. In just a couple of weeks or so," Jack said.

"It's September?" Tom asked. "We lost track of time since we've been up here."

"Yessir, it's mid September, actually," Jack said. "It won't be long till the snow hits. It always comes early up here in the mountains. And when it comes, you don't get out till spring."

"We really need to get to town soon then," Emily said.

"I'd say so, young lady. The sooner, the better."

The evening wrapped up and before long, Emily was yawning and starting to nod off.

"I think it's time for bed," Tom said. "We get up early in the morning to get our chores done."

"I'm an early riser too," said Jack. "So I'll say good night to you three and hit the hay."

Jack headed for Nellie's bedroom and let the curtain drop behind him.

Tom checked the door and made sure it was locked and pulled Emily aside. "I don't want you or Mercy coming down during the night for anything, ok?"

"Why not?" Emily asked.

"Cause I don't, ok?"

"Ok, fine, but what if I have to use the outhouse?"

"Use the slop bucket."

"Ewww, you know I hate using that. I'm always the one who has to clean them out in the morning."

"Em, please. I'm just trying to protect you."

"From what?"

"We don't know Jack very well. I just don't want you coming down here unless you're fully dressed and I'm awake."

Emily blinked several times in confusion. "Is something wrong, Tom?"

"I just want to keep you and Mercy safe, is all."

Emily realized he was just looking out for her and she suddenly felt a lot safer cause of this. She threw her arms around him and hugged him tight. "Thank you, Tom."

"Hey, it's my job to watch out for you and Mercy. You heard Jack. You're my womenfolk and it's my job."

Emily released him and gave him a big smile. She quickly turned and climbed the ladder to the loft. Mercy had already climbed up and was settling into the bed. "Wha did Tom wanna talk ta ya 'bout?"

"He doesn't want us to go downstairs during the night. He says he's protecting us."

"Mmhmm," Mercy said.

"What? What does that mean?"

"It means he likes ya an' wants ta make sho yous safe."

"He doesn't want you to go down either," Emily said.

"I never does," Mercy said. "Yous da on'y one who does. I jus use da pot."

"Oh Mercy," Emily said. "You're making more out of it than there is."

"I don tink so. Tom likes ya."

"He likes you too."

"Not da same wayyyy," Mercy sang out.

"Oh hush now and go to sleep."

Emily flopped over onto her side with her back to Mercy. Mercy just laid there and giggled until Emily rolled back over and began to giggle too.

"Do you really think he likes me?"

"O' course I does. I sees da way he looks at ya."

Emily giggled again. "Can I tell you a little secret?"

"Sho."

"I kinda like him too."

"Tole ya."

Both girls broke out into giggles again until Tom called up for them to be quiet and go to sleep.

Emily snuggled down into the covers with a smile on her face. Maybe Tom did like her. More than as a sister? Maybe as a girlfriend?

As she lay there in the dark, her thoughts were on Tom. *I wonder if I'll marry him someday,* was the last thought she had as she drifted off to sleep.

CHAPTER 19

The next few days were spent learning as much from Jack as they could. He taught Tom how to use a gun and made him practice with it till he was able to hit the target every time.

Jack showed Tom how to harness up the horses and wagon and gave him instructions on how the drive the team. He also showed him the proper way to care for the horses during the winter months.

Mercy stayed clear of Jack as much as possible. She knew how to do her chores and didn't need no man telling her how to do them. She fixed everyone's dinner each night and cleaned up the kitchen when they were done. She didn't join in with the talk at the table much either. She was beginning to feel out of place and preferred to go off quietly by herself after the meals were done.

Jack showed Emily an easy way to do the laundry which would save her hands from all the blisters she kept getting. He showed her how to mend clothing and to do basic sewing. She enjoyed her time with him. He told her stories of how his mama had taught him how to sew, knit and mend along with all the other household chores he would need to know in order to live by himself.

A week passed and Jack announced that he would have to be heading home in the morning.

"Awww, do you have to go?" Emily asked.

"Afraid so, young'un," said Jack. "I've got to get my place ready for the long winter months that are coming."

"We're going to miss you, Jack," Tom said.

Emily noticed that once again, Mercy had disappeared up to the loft once dinner was over.

Climbing up the ladder, she found Mercy curled up on the bed. "What's wrong, Mercy?"

"Nuffin."

"Why aren't you downstairs with the rest of us?"

"Din't wanna be."

"Why? Are you feeling sick?"

"Nah."

"Mercy..." Emily said. "Is something wrong? Are you mad at me?"

"I don belong down dere wiff ya guys."

"What are you talking about? Of course you belong with us."

"I's da on'y blackie."

"So? You've been the only one since we met."

"I jus feel like I don belong."

"Well, you're wrong. You belong with me no matter what. I love you, Mercy."

"Ya does?"

"Of course, I do."

Mercy sat up in the bed and wiped a tear from her cheek. "Yo an' Tom seem so happy wif Jack dat I tot mebbe I was jus a burden."

"You could never be a burden to me," Emily said, pulling her into a hug. "You're my sister, remember?"

"I's jus a bit jealous o' Jack I guess. Yous spendin' so much time wif 'im and not me."

"Oh Mercy, I'm so sorry. I was just enjoying all the stories he was telling."

"Em, I don tink I wanna leave dis cabin come springtime."

"Why not? Don't you want to go home?"

"Em…," Mercy said. "I is home."

Emily didn't know what to say. She certainly enjoyed being here with Tom and Mercy, but she never gave up the hope of going home to her father. A deep sadness filled her heart. Would she be able to stay here forever with just Mercy and Tom?

"It's, ok Mercy," she said. "We'll talk about this with Tom once Jack leaves."

Mercy nodded her head and curled up on her side again. Emily knew she wouldn't come back down stairs, so she went down alone.

Jack and Tom were sitting in front of the fireplace while Jack was teaching Tom how to whittle. Emily took a seat on the floor and watched, but her mind was far away.

The next morning, Jack hitched up his horse and wagon and bade farewell to the kids. Tom hated to see him go. He had learned so much from him that he would miss having him around.

Emily had enjoyed his visit, but she was really worried about Mercy and knew that until Jack left, they couldn't talk about it.

As Jack pulled out of the yard and headed on his way, Tom turned to Emily. "Ok, so tell me. What's going on with Mercy?"

Emily told him about the conversation she had had with Mercy the night before and Tom just shook his head. "Well, that's just crazy," he said. "She does belong with us and always will."

"I know, but I think she's starting to feel left out or something."

Tom ran inside and climbed the ladder to the loft. Mercy was still in bed and had not come down to say goodbye to Jack.

Emily stayed downstairs and let Tom talk to her alone. After several minutes, Tom called Emily up.

"Seems Mercy is feeling like we're going to ditch her along the way," he told Emily when she joined them.

"What? Why?" Emily asked, completely shocked.

"She thinks that since we have certain feelings for each other, that we are not going to want her around anymore."

Emily was shocked by this revelation. Tom had feelings for her too? Gathering her thoughts, she quickly threw herself down on the bed next to Mercy.

"Now you listen here," she said, firmly. "Just because Tom and I may have feelings for each other doesn't mean we would ever, and I mean ever, want you to leave. You are our family and always will be, got it?"

Mercy rubbed her eyes and sat up. "I's jus afeared dat I might git in da way."

"No way," Tom said. "It's the three of us all the way. Forever."

"Ya mean it?" Mercy asked.

"Yes!" Tom and Emily said together.

"I love ya guys," Mercy said between hiccups. She dried her eyes and hugged each of them in turn.

"Now, we need to see about a trip to town," Tom said.

"Nellie always left early in the morning," Emily said. "It's too late to leave today."

"I agree," said Tom. "We will get up early and leave just before dawn."

"I'll git a lunch prepared ta take wif us," Mercy said.

"Good idea," said Tom. "So it's planned then. We leave in the morning. Now, let's get our chores done."

They scrambled off the bed and each got busy with their assigned chores.

Emily's chore was the laundry. She rounded up all the dirty clothes and set up the tub of water, along with the washboard, out in the front yard. They had discovered a clothesline stretching between two trees out behind the house. Once she had scrubbed and rinsed the clothes and wrung them out, she threw them into the basket beside her.

As she worked, she listened to all the sounds the mountain around her made. She could hear birds twittering in the trees and the occasional snort of one of the horses in the barn. She began to hum a little tune that Olive used to sing to her. Her mind was on their upcoming trip to town when she suddenly realized everything had gotten quiet. She looked up from her chore, but nothing seemed out of the ordinary. She began humming again when she suddenly heard what sounded like a woman screaming.

She jumped to her feet just as Tom stuck his head out of the barn. "Was that you?" he asked Emily.

"No."

"What was it then?"

Emily looked around the yard and shook her head. "I have no idea. Where's Mercy?"

The scream came again, only louder and closer. Tom took off for the house looking for Mercy. He found her in the kitchen rolling out biscuits for dinner. "Did you scream?" he asked her.

"Nah, why?" she asked.

"We heard a woman scream outside."

Mercy dropped the biscuit she was holding and ran outside. "Emily, git in da house, now!" she yelled to Emily.

Emily was still sitting on the ground wringing out clothes when Mercy yelled for her. "Why? What's wrong?"

"Dat's not a woman. Dat's a mountain lion. Git in here now!" Mercy yelled frantically at her.

Emily had just managed to get to her feet when she suddenly felt a sharp pain radiate up the back of her leg. She let out a scream as she was knocked to the ground by something big and hairy that she hadn't even seen coming.

"Emily!" Tom yelled. He turned around and disappeared back into the cabin. He returned carrying the rifle that Jack had taught him how to use.

Emily could smell the rancid breath of the big cat that was sitting on her as it breathed down her neck. It flexed it's claws which dug into the tender flesh on her back. She let out a cry and the cat screamed back. The sounds pierced Emily's ears, deafening her momentarily. Saliva from the cat's jaws dribbled down onto her neck and the cat suddenly bit down on the back of her head. She had wrapped her braided hair up into a bun while she was working and the cat had managed to miss her scalp, but had latched onto the bun instead. It shook it's huge head violently from side to side, jerking Emily's head around. She screamed again.

A loud *thwack* split the air and the cat instantly let go of her bun and slumped onto the ground beside her.

She lay there for several moments afraid to move. Her left leg was burning terribly and her head and neck ached from the shaking the cat had done. She didn't notice the pain in her back, even though she knew she had been clawed.

Tom and Mercy rushed out to her. Tom poked the cat with the butt of the rifle to make sure it was dead. It didn't move. He then dropped onto his knees next to Emily and rolled her over. "Are you ok?" he asked, concern etched on his face.

"I don't know," Emily said. "My leg hurts. My head hurts."

Mercy rushed inside and came back out with a towel. "Yous bleedin', Em," she said, as she mopped up the blood from Emily's leg. "He got ya good."

Tom lifted her into his arms and carried her into the house. He gently laid her on the divan and began to examine her wounds.

"We need to get these cleaned up," he told Mercy. "Go get some water and some old rags. See if you can find any medicine."

Mercy ran to the kitchen and grabbed a bucket and took it outside to the well to fill it up with water. She returned and dropped the bucket next to Tom's feet. She then rummaged around in the kitchen till she found something she thought might be medicine. Bringing it to Tom, she handed it to him.

"What's this?" he asked her. It looked like some kind of salve, but the label on it was so badly faded, it wasn't able to be read.

"I tink it's a herbal salve," Mercy said.

Tom began washing off the bite on the back of Emily's leg. The puncture wounds were deep and were bleeding heavily. Using a cloth Mercy had brought him, he applied pressure till the bleeding slowed down. He then smeared some of the unidentified salve into the wounds.

Emily moaned, but didn't protest. Her whole body hurt. She was scared to open her eyes for fear of how bad the wounds were.

"I need to see your back, Em," Tom said, as he gently rolled her over. He began unbuttoning her dress, but Mercy stopped him.

"Tom, lemme do it," she said. "Yous not s'posed ta see her half naked."

Tom stepped aside and let Mercy take over. She finished unbuttoning Emily's dress and slid it down off her shoulders. The claw punctures weren't that bad. They had just broken the surface of her skin. Mercy cleaned them up and smeared some of the salve onto those wounds as well.

Once Emily had been cleaned up and her dress pulled back over her shoulders, she scooted up to a sitting position. She pulled the rag that was wrapped around her leg back and inspected the wound. The holes were deep and blood still oozed out of them. It ran down her leg mingled with the salve. She quickly wrapped the rag back around her leg and looked up at Tom with fear in her eyes. "What are we going to do if this gets infected?"

"We need to get you to a doctor," Tom said. "We'll have to wait till morning as planned though."

"What happened to the mountain lion?"

"I shot him," Tom said. "He's dead."

Emily suddenly began to cry. The adrenaline had worn off and fear overtook her. She began shaking and broke out in a cold sweat.

"We needs ta git her wrapped up in a blanket," Mercy said.

Tom grabbed the blanket off the back of the divan and wrapped it around Emily. He pulled her up next to him and held her tight, waiting for the shaking to subside.

"I think she needs to stay in bed for the rest of the day," Tom said.

He laid her down on the divan and tucked the blanket around her. "One of us will stay with her, while the other one finishes up the chores," Tom said.

"I's gonna sit wif her. Ya can go finish up da chores. I can keep an eye on her while I git dinner ready."

Tom agreed and headed outside to finish up his chores. He didn't know what to do with the dead cat, so he drug it out behind the house and buried it.

Mercy sat by Emily's side till it was time to fix dinner. Emily slept most of the time. Her head was pounding and her whole body throbbed. She didn't want to move and wouldn't accept the water that Mercy kept trying to get her to drink.

When dinner was ready, Mercy took Emily a plate, but she wouldn't eat it, so Mercy just left her alone to rest.

As nighttime approached, Emily's leg was beginning to ache and hurt pretty bad. She pulled the rag off and saw that it was soaked with blood.

"Mercy," she called. "I need another rag, please."

Mercy grabbed another rag and brought it over to her. She knelt down on the floor next to her and looked at the wound. "Dat looks really bad, Em," she said, wrapping the clean rag around Emily's leg.

"I know," said Emily. "It really hurts too."

"We's gonna git ya ta da doctor tomorrie ta see 'bout it."

"Mercy? How did you know that was a mountain lion and not a woman?"

"My mama tole me 'bout dem. She used ta say dat when she was a slave down in Souf Carolina, dat sometimes when dey's out in da field, dey would hear what dey tot was a woman screamin', but it was a mountain lion. She tole me dey was very dangerous and iffn dey heared one, dey all ran fo da house."

"She was right," Emily said. "They are dangerous."

"Well, Tom don took care o' dat one. He ain't gonna hurt no one no more."

"I'm glad Tom was here. I'm glad Jack taught him how to use a gun."

"Me too," Mercy said. "It's kinda nice ta has a man around."

Emily giggled at that and Mercy joined in.

"We need one for you," Emily said.

"One wha? A man? Yous crazy, Em. Jus plain crazy."

Emily was feeling a little bit better, other than the pain in her leg, and decided she needed something to eat. Mercy brought her a couple of biscuits and a small chunk of cheese.

As Emily ate, she remembered something Mercy had said the day before.

"Mercy?" she asked. "What did you mean when you said you were home. You told me that when we were talking yesterday."

Mercy looked down at her lap and let out a long sigh. "I meaned dat dis farm is my home now."

"But what about Ohio? Your mother? Or Pennsylvania, with me?"

"Em, I never tole ya dis afore, but iffn I's ta go back up Norf, I'd haf ta go wif ya ta Pennsylvanie. I wouldna be able ta goes ta Ohio."

"What? Why? I mean, I would love for you to come live with me. I've wanted you to all along, but why couldn't you go back to your mother?"

"I's a burden ta my modder. She din't want me. Never did. She got pregnant by accident and she tole me I made her life harder. She kept me cause she had ta, not cause she wanted ta. Iffn I's ta go back, she wone want me and prolly wone let me stay now."

"Oh Mercy, how horrible. Why didn't you tell me this before?"

"Din't know how ta tell ya, I guess. I love my mama, but she din't love me back."

"Well, then it's a good thing that we already have plans for you to come home with me then, huh?"

"Em, I's not sho I wanna leave dis place," Mercy said quietly.

"You don't want to go home with me?"

"It's not dat. But I's a blackie. I's not gonna fit in wif yo family. I's always gonna be an outsider dere. Here, I don haf ta worry 'bout dat. I can stay here on dis mountain and nobody gonna care. I's accepted in dat town too. I loves it here."

"So if I leave in the spring, you're not going to come with me?"

"No, Em. I's home righ' here." Mercy bowed her head again and rubbed her hands together. "I's sorry Em. But I belong here."

Emily couldn't believe what she was hearing. She didn't want to make the journey without Mercy. Mercy was her best friend. Her sister. A deep sadness fell over her. She grabbed Mercy's hand and squeezed. "I guess I don't understand what's it's like to be colored, but I sure don't want to go without you. I'll miss you something awful."

They sat beside each other, but never said a word. A silent tear ran down Emily's face.

Tom came in and saw the girls sitting on the divan together. He knew immediately that something was wrong. "What's going on guys?" he asked, coming over to sit with them on the couch.

"Mercy is going to stay here," Emily said.

"We need you to come tomorrow, Mercy," Tom said. "I may need help with something and Emily won't be able to help."

"Not tomorrow, Tom," Emily said. "She won't be leaving with us come spring."

"Oh. Why not?"

"She wants to stay here."

Mercy lifted her eyes to Tom's and hoped for understanding. He reached over and patted her on the knee. "I think I understand," he said. "You can live peacefully here, where in a big town or around white folk, you may have troubles. Is that right?"

Mercy nodded her head, but didn't say anything.

"Well, I too would prefer to stay here," Tom said. "I've never had a real home. This is the first real place I could call home."

"So you're going to stay here too?" Emily asked.

"I don't know, Emily," Tom replied. "Spring is a long way off. A lot can happen between now and then. Let's just get through the winter and see what happens."

Emily felt panic well up inside her. She wouldn't be able to make that journey by herself. It was too far. She was afraid. She had been counting on making the trip with her friends. Now what was she going to do? Her head began to throb in earnest.

"I'm tired," she said. She turned away from them and curled up on her side. "I'm just going to go to sleep now."

Tom and Mercy left her laying on the divan. Neither of them knew what to say to her. They finished cleaning up the kitchen together, then got ready for bed. Since Emily was on the divan and Mercy headed up for the loft, Tom decided to sleep in Nellie's bed. He gave Emily one last look, then dropped the curtain behind him. He didn't know how to tell her that he desperately wanted her to stay at the cabin forever too.

CHAPTER 20

Emily was roused from her sleep before the sun was even up. She rolled over and saw Tom holding a lantern leaning over her.

"Time to get up, Sleepy Head," he said to her.

She rolled over and felt a sharp stab of pain rip up the back of her leg. She sat up quickly and pulled the rag off of her leg to look at the wound. It was red and swollen, but it wasn't bleeding. Tom held the lantern down to get a better look at it.

"It stopped bleeding," he said. "That's a good sign."

"Yes, I suppose it is," Emily said. She was still upset about the conversation the three of them had the night before and didn't really feel like talking much.

She quickly swung her legs around and put her feet on the floor. "I need to get ready to go," she said, preparing to stand up. Tom grabbed her arm to steady her. She rose to her feet and tested whether or not she could put weight on her bad leg. It ached and hurt, but she was able to stand on it.

"It's good that you can stand, too," Tom said. She could tell he was uncomfortable this morning as well. She wondered if the talk had caused him any concern. By the way he was acting, she assumed it had.

"Just go get the horses and wagon ready," she told him. "I'm ok. I'm just going to go get ready and I'll be out."

Tom released her arm and headed for the door. He glanced up to the loft and knocked on the ladder. "Come on, Mercy," he said. "Time to get going."

Emily heard Mercy ruffling around upstairs, but didn't give it any of her attention. She didn't know what to say to Mercy. She was hurting inside and didn't know what to do about it. She just needed time to understand Mercy's decision and to think about what she would do about it.

A half hour later, Tom had the horses hitched up and had thrown a couple of blankets in the back for Emily. He grabbed the jar of money and stuffed a wad of it into his trousers.

Mercy had prepared a lunch of bread, cheese and dried jerky to take with them. She stuffed it into a small satchel she had found under Nellie's bed and tossed it into the back of the wagon.

Tom helped Emily into the back of the wagon and took his seat at the reins. The rifle was laid across the floorboards at his feet.

Mercy joined Tom up on the seat, leaving Emily in the back all alone.

Emily was glad they chose to sit up there away from her. She needed time to think. She needed time to get over her hurt. She loved the mountain as much as they did, but what about her father? She couldn't let him always wonder what had happened to her. She missed him and knew he was probably worried sick. She just couldn't stay here and forget about him.

Tom steered the horses toward the road and they headed off toward the town.

The horses didn't need steered. They seemed to know exactly where they were going and Emily remembered that Nellie had told them that the horses knew their way to and from the town.

The sun eventually broke the horizon. A beautiful display of blues and purples touched the mountaintop as the sun rose steadily in the sky. Clouds obscured the distance mountains with their blue, hazy blanket. The air was chilly and the smell of pine floated by on a breeze.

Emily sat up and took in all the beauty around her. It truly was majestic here. She would love for her father to see this. She sniffed the air and savored the clean, fresh scent of it.

They eventually reached the part of the trail that made a steep descent. Tom gave the horses their heads and just sat back in the seat and let them navigate their own way down.

It took hours for them to reach the town. Emily guessed it was probably late morning by the time they rolled in. Tom stopped the horses in front of the mercantile and jumped down from the wagon.

"I'm going to go see Sam and find out where we can find the doctor," he said. "After we get Emily taken care of, then we'll worry about the supplies."

Sam saw them pull up and came out to greet them. He informed them that Bessie was working at the restaurant and would be happy to see them.

After pointing them to the doctor's office, he took the supply list from Tom and told them he would get everything rounded up for them while they attended to Emily.

The doctor was in his office when Tom opened the door and ushered Emily in.

"What have we here?" the doctor asked. He was a short, plump man with a warm smile and kind eyes.

"She was attacked by a mountain lion," Tom told him.

The doctor quickly assisted Emily through a door into a room just off the entrance and helped her up onto an exam table. Tom and Mercy followed them into the room.

"You two will have to wait outside while I exam her," the doctor told them. "Shoo now." He turned to Emily and said, "I'm Doctors Stevens. And who would you be?"

"I'm Emily, sir."

"Well, tell me what happened and then show me your wounds."

Emily told him how the lion had come out of nowhere and bit her leg and jumped on her back.

The doctor quickly got to work examining her bruises and checking her for a fever or other symptoms she might have.

"Where are your folks, young lady?" he asked as he poured some antiseptic on her leg.

Emily explained the situation to him. From how she was kidnapped, to how they ended up at the cabin all alone.

"Well, I'll be," he said. "You sure are brave kids."

"I just wish I could let my father know what happened and where I am," Emily told him.

"Well, have you considered sending him a telegram?"

"A what, sir?"

"A telegram. There's a telegram machine at the post office just down the street." He explained to her how it worked and that she could send a message just about anywhere she needed one sent.

Emily's ears began ringing. There was a way to let her father know where she was? Why had no one told her this before? Hope rose in her like a huge wave. If her father knew where she was, he could come get her. She wouldn't have to travel home all by herself come spring.

The doctor finished cleaning up Emily's cuts and bruises and smeared some sweet smelling salve on her leg, then wrapped it tightly with some bandages. "There you go, young lady," he said. "All done."

The doctor called Tom and Mercy in and explained to them that Emily's leg was not infected due, in part, to the thorough cleaning job they had done on it. He told them that the salve they had used was indeed a healing salve that he had given to Nellie several months back when she had gotten a cut on her leg. He gave Emily some powder for pain and some fresh bandages and sent them on their way.

As they left the doctor's office, Emily told them about the telegram she wanted to send to her father.

"Do we have enough money to send one, Tom?" she asked hopefully.

"Yes, we should," Tom said. He pulled the money out of his trouser pocket and counted what he had. "We should have plenty to pay for our supplies and the telegram."

They made their way down the street to the post office. Emily limped along, but was so excited about sending her father a message, that she didn't feel the discomfort in her leg.

When they reached the post office, Emily explained to the clerk what she wanted. He drew out a sheet of paper from under the desk and wrote down what Emily wanted to say and took the address of her father's house in Pennsylvania.

"It could takes weeks for this to reach him and then we will have to wait for a response," he told Emily. "Hopefully the next time you come into town, we'll have an answering telegram for you."

"We probably won't be back until springtime," Emily said, disheartened. "We'll be snowed in till then."

"I'm sorry, little lady," the clerk said. "There's nothing I can do about the weather."

"It's ok, Emily," Tom said. "At least when he gets your message, he'll know you're ok."

Emily agreed. She paid the fee and thanked the clerk, then the three of them walked out of the post office and down the street toward the mercantile.

"Em," Mercy said. "Dat's great dat yous able ta send 'im a message. Mebbe iffn he knows where ya be, he can come git ya."

"I hope so," Emily said. She didn't want to let the idea that it would be months before she got word back dampen her spirits, so she forced a smile on her face and hobbled down the street with them to the mercantile.

Sam had informed Bessie that the kids were in town, so she was waiting for them outside the mercantile and invited them to lunch before they headed back up the mountain.

Sitting around the table with Sam and Bessie, Emily recounted everything that had happened since they left with Nellie only a couple weeks prior.

"Poor Nellie," Bessie said. "God rest her soul. I know she'd be happy to be reunited with Frank again, though."

They all agreed and talk turned to the upcoming winter.

"I've packed a few extra supplies for you kids that you'll need during the winter," Sam said. "Candles, fuel for lanterns, extra dry goods and some extra bullets for that rifle."

"We don't have enough money to pay for all that," Tom protested.

"Ah, don't worry about that," Sam said. "I'm throwing it all in at no charge."

"Thank you," Emily said.

"You guys will need coats, mittens and hats, too," said Bessie. "I'll cover those for you down at the tailor's."

They finished their meals and headed off for the tailor shop with Bessie. She purchased them each a heavy coat, mittens and a hat. She insisted that Mercy get a pair of boots as well. She reluctantly agreed and those were added to the stack of items as well.

When they returned to the mercantile, Sam had all their supplies gathered up and stacked outside the door waiting for them.

Sam and Tom began loading the supplies into the wagon as Bessie, Emily and Mercy said their goodbyes.

"Oh, by the way," Tom asked. "Whatever happened to Mr. Guthrie?"

Sam and Bessie exchanged glances.

"He was released," Bessie said. "The judge who came through town said he didn't have enough evidence to convict him, so he let him go."

"What?" Emily exclaimed. "How could he do that?"

"With you guys out of town, there wasn't anyone to testify against him," Sam said. "We told him what happened outside of the church building, but he said it wasn't enough to put him in jail for. I'm so sorry. We tried."

Fresh fear crept up Emily's spine. Would he still be out there searching for them or would he just give up and go back to wherever it was he came from?

"Does 'e knowed where we are?" Mercy asked.

"We don't think so," Bessie said. "When he left, he headed out of town, so we just assumed he would probably just keep on going."

"I sure hope so," Emily said. A shiver ran up her spine. The thought that he was still out there unnerved her.

They all said their goodbyes and the three of them began their journey back up the mountain.

The trip back was a solemn one. The thought that Mr. Guthrie was out there, possibly still hunting for them, weighed heavily on their minds. He threatened to keep searching for them. Would he?

They arrived back at the cabin just as the sun was beginning to set. The air was considerably more chilly now then when they had left that morning. The sky seemed to be turning an odd shade of gray and heavy fog was starting to settle over the farm.

Tom helped the girls unload the wagon and got the horses brushed down and in their stalls, just as the first snowflakes began to fall.

CHAPTER 21

Snow blanketed the mountaintop. The landscape looked like millions of diamonds sprinkled everywhere. The air was cold and crisp and snowflakes whirled through the air whenever the wind blew.

Emily gazed out the window at the winter wonderland that stretched out as far as the eye could see.

"Have you ever seen anything more beautiful?" she asked Tom and Mercy.

"Nah sirree," said Mercy, coming to stand next to her. Together their breath fogged up the window.

Tom threw another couple of logs on the fire and poked around in the embers to encourage a bigger blaze. "Can't say that I have," he said. "I think we should go out for a walk and enjoy some fresh air."

It had been a few weeks since they had returned from town and snow had fallen almost everyday.

Sam had given them a calendar while they were at the mercantile. Tom walked over to where it hung on the wall and drew a line through the date with a pencil he had tied to the tack it hung from. He was trying to keep track of the days and months. It was easy to lose all track of time up here on the mountain and he felt it was important to know what month it was and what day.

"Hey," he called to the girls who were still gazing out the window. "You know what today is?

"October something," Emily said.

"October thirteenth," he said.

Mercy's mouth dropped open and she turned to Emily. "T'day's our birfday!"

Since Emily's and Mercy's birthdays were both in October, they decided to share a day to celebrate. Emily's birthday was on the seventeenth and Mercy's was on the ninth, so they split it in the middle and chose that date to celebrate.

"I's gonna haf ta git a cake baked fo us," Mercy said.

"I can't believe we're going to be fourteen years old," Emily said, excitedly.

"It's still early," Tom said. "Why don't you get the cake baked, then we can head out for a walk. What do you say?"

The girls both agreed and Mercy got busy whipping up the cake while Emily tidied up the house.

Tom cleaned the rifle the way Jack had shown him, then loaded it and set it by the door. They never left the house without it ever since Emily was attacked by the mountain lion. Her wounds had all healed, but she would have scars on her leg from the bite wound.

After the cake had baked, Mercy pulled it out and set it on the table to cool. It turned out mighty fine if she did say so herself.

Emily and Mercy borrowed some of Tom's pants whenever they went out in the snow. It didn't make any sense to wear a dress since their legs would freeze.

Wrapping their coats tightly around themselves and stuffing their feet into their boots, the three of them stepped out into the snow.

Tom made sure to keep a path cleared from the house to the barn, but the rest of the place was piled up deep.

They trudged through the knee-high snow past the barn and off into the woods that surrounded the farm. They had discovered a path that took them passed tall rock ledges, over little babbling creeks, past pine forests and along tree canopied trails. It was one of their favorite spots to hike to get out of the cabin for awhile.

Emily was used to snow, being from Pennsylvania, but the snow here on the mountain was deeper, thicker and heavier than what she was used to. It coated the trees and clung to the sides of the rock ledges. She had to catch her breath sometimes at the sight of it. On days like this when they went for a stroll through the woods, she could almost forget about her home in Pennsylvania...almost.

They picked their way through the trees for awhile when Tom suddenly stopped them.

"Do you smell smoke?" he asked.

Emily sniffed the air, but didn't smell anything. "No."

"I's not smellin' nuffin but snow," Mercy said.

Emily giggled and said, "You can't smell snow, silly."

"I can," Mercy said. "It smells cold."

The three of them laughed and continued on their way.

They were a good distance from the cabin, when they decided to turn around and head back.

"I'm starting to get cold," Tom said. "My feet are wet too."

"I's bin cold," Mercy said. "I seys we turn 'round an' heads back."

"Me too," Emily said. Even though she had mittens on, her hands were getting numb and were beginning to ache.

Suddenly the faint smell of smoke wafted over them.

"There it is again," Tom said. "Smoke."

Emily and Mercy could both smell it now and looked around them in every direction looking for the source of it.

"I smell it too," Emily said.

"Me too," said Mercy.

"Let's go see if we can find where it's coming from," Tom said.

He walked a bit farther up the trail when he saw smoke curling up out of a small cave entrance just off the side of the path.

"There's someone in that cave," he told the girls.

"I bet it's Jack," Emily said. She stepped around Tom and began heading toward the small cave.

"Em, wait," Mercy warned. "Wha' if it's not Jack."

"Who else would it be way up here?" Emily asked. "We're miles from anywhere. It has to be Jack."

"Let me go first, Emily," Tom said. "I have the gun in case it's not Jack."

Emily saw the wisdom in Tom's words and stepped aside to let him go first. She had come to trust Tom when he told her not to do something. He was always looking out for her and Mercy and it warmed her heart to know he cared so much.

Tom slowly crept up the path toward the cave. He had the gun held out in front of him with his finger near the trigger in case he had to use it.

They reached the cave entrance and Tom stuck his head inside the opening. Looking around, he didn't see anyone, but set back in just a short ways was the source of the smoke. A small fire had been lit and a stack of wood was piled beside it.

He turned around to say something to the girls, when we was suddenly whacked with a large branch across his back.

Emily heard the sickening thud and let out a scream as Mercy jumped forward and tackled the person holding the branch and fell to the ground on top of him.

Tom quickly got to his feet, rubbing his lower back with his hand. The gun had gone flying when he fell and was laying several feet off to the side. He quickly grabbed it up and turned to see how had hit him.

Emily stood frozen on the spot as she watched Mercy scramble to her feet. On the ground in front of her lay a young man. He was dirty and his clothes were rumpled and shredded. He was barefoot and covered in cuts and bruises.

"Who ya be?" Mercy demanded of him.

"Who is you?" the young man asked in return.

Emily just stared at him waiting for an answer.

Tom held the gun up and pointed it at him. "I believe she asked you a question," he said.

The young man eyed the gun, then turned his gaze to Mercy. "Name's Jed...Jedediah."

Mercy eyed the young man and slowly relaxed her posture. "I's Mercy," she said, holding out her hand for him to shake.

He got to his feet and ignoring Mercy's hand, studied the three of them. "What's ya'll doin' out in dese woods," he asked, directing his question at Tom.

"We live out here," Tom said. "What are you doing out here. You don't even have a coat on."

Mercy continued to stare at him. He was about Tom's age, she figured. He was tall with black skin and short, curly hair. Mercy thought he was the best looking young man she had ever seen.

"Ya'll lives out here? In da woods?"

"In a cabin not far from here," Tom replied.

"Why's ya in dis cave, Jed," Mercy asked.

Jed looked around nervously. "Anyone else wif ya'll?"

"No, it's just us," Tom said.

"Well, I figger I ain't got nuffin ta lose by tellin' ya," Jed said. "I's runnin' from some'un."

"Who," Emily asked.

"His name's Guffrie," Jed said.

Emily and Mercy both gasped.

"You mean, Mr. Guthrie?" Tom asked.

"Yeah, dat's him," said Jed.

"He kidnapped you too," Emily asked.

"Yeah. An' he tryin' ta take me ta Souf Carolina to some auction down dere."

Mercy's legs gave out on her and she slumped to the ground. "He takes boys too den," she said, just barely above a whisper. "I never seen no boys wif 'im. Jus us girls."

"He nabbed ya too?" Jed asked Mercy.

"Me and Em bofe," Mercy said.

"How did you end up out here on this mountain?" Tom asked.

"Don rightly know," Jed said. "We'd bin traveling fo a long way and I saws an opp'tunity to hightail it, so's I took it. I bin out here fo days. I foun' dis cave and bin campin' out here ever since."

"Tom, we need to get him back to the cabin and warm him up," Emily said. "He's lucky he hasn't froze to death."

"Would you like to come home with us?" Tom asked.

"You bet," Jed said.

He extinguished the fire and followed them back to the cabin. He was shivering and by the time they reached the cabin, and he had snow caked to his feet and pant legs.

When they opened the door, Jed bolted over to the fire and threw himself onto the floor in front of it. Tom got to work building up the fire so a good, strong blaze burned.

Emily grabbed a blanket off Tom's bed and handed it to Jed. Wrapping it around himself, he thanked her.

Mercy put some water in the kettle over the fire and when it boiled, she made everyone a hot cup of tea.

They sat around the fire with Jed until they were sure he was warmed up and dry.

"I can't tank you'uns enuf," he told them. "Iffn I's ta stay out dere any longer, I's sho I'd a froze ta deaf."

"So tell us what happened," Emily said. "Where are you from? How did you end up with Mr. Guthrie? Where is he now?"

"I've from Norf Kentucky. I's a freed slave, ya see. I's workin' fo ole man McClure when one dey dis man comes up ta me and tells me he has sumpin fo Mr. McClure dat he needs me ta take ta him. So I follows along affer 'im and nex' ting I knows, I's bein' tied up and hauled off. Nex' ting I knows is I's in Norf Carolina and Mr. Guffrie tells me he takin' me souf to be auctioned off to a slave owner. One night when ever'one was sleepin' I managed ta free myself and I jus' took off runnin' and never looked back. I din't stop till I finds dat cave."

"How long have you been out there?" Emily asked.

"Don know fo sho. Seems like fo'ever."

"Well, yous safe now, Jed," Mercy said. "Yous welcome ta stays here wif us, right guys?" she asked Tom and Emily.

"Absolutely," Tom said. "But we will need to go over some rules and such with you. We all have chores around here and everyone pitches in."

"I's pufectly fine wif dat," Jed said. "I's use ta hard work. I's jus happy ta has a place ta stay dat ain't in no cave."

"It's settled then," Tom said. "Welcome to the family."

"Family?" Jed asked. "Wha' ya mean?"

"The three of us are family," Emily explained. "Now that you are going to be staying with us, you will be family, too."

"I like dat," Jed said. A smile spread across his face and he nodded his head. "Yeah, I like dat."

Tom, Emily and Mercy took turns telling Jed the rules and laying out the chores that had to be done every day. He readily agreed to help Tom with the horses, cutting wood and whatever else Tom needed help with. He informed them that he was a really good hunter and would teach Tom how to kill a deer for meat. Tom was happy to have someone around who could help out with the chores. Sometimes it got lonely being the only man around. Especially since the girls spent so much time alone together without him.

Mercy bustled around the kitchen getting dinner ready while Emily prepared the divan for Jed to sleep on. Since Tom had finally taken Nellie's old room as his own, it left the divan as the only available spot for Jed to sleep.

Tom spent that time getting to know Jed better. Emily noticed that the two of them seemed to really hit it off as friends. It reminded her of how easily she and Mercy had become friends. She smiled at the memory.

They sat around the small table and ate their dinner. Jed crammed his food in his mouth like he was starving. Emily looked at Mercy and winked. They both remembered what it felt like to be hungry. Emily gave a quick prayer of thanksgiving for all they had now.

When the meal was over and the dishes cleaned up, Mercy carried the cake over and placed it in the middle of the table.

"Today is Emily's and Mercy's birthdays," Tom explained to him. "Mercy made a cake to celebrate."

Mercy cut the cake into four large pieces and laid them on plates for each of them.

Tom and Jed sang '*Happy Birthday*' to them as they ate their cake.

When evening came around, Tom went in to the chest in his room and removed a set of clothes. He came out and handed them to Jed. "You look like you're about my size, so these should fit you."

Jed gratefully took the clothes and slipped behind the curtain to change. When he stepped back out, Tom noticed that the clothes fit him perfectly.

"How old are you, Jed?" Tom asked him.

"I's almos' sixteen years ole," Jed answered him.

Mercy couldn't take her eyes off Jed. She looked him up and down and was suddenly very glad that he had come to stay with them.

That night as she and Emily snuggled down into their bed, Mercy couldn't keep her excitement contained any longer.

"He sho is good lookin'," she told Emily.

"Jed?"

"Yup."

"You really like him, don't you?"

"Yup."

Emily giggled and tickled Mercy's ribs. "You have a crush on him, just like I do for Tom."

Mercy giggled. "Yup."

CHAPTER 22

The next several months passed by uneventfully. Snow blanketed the mountaintop and the temperatures were below freezing most of the time. The long days and nights were spent huddled indoors around the fire.

The four of them had fallen into the daily routine of chores, then in the evening, they would sit around the fire and talk or piece together an old puzzle they had found in the bottom of Nellie's chest.

Jed turned out to be a hard worker and very eager to help with anything that needed done. He was very easy going and kind. He repeatedly apologized to Tom for hitting him with the branch the first day they met, but explained that he thought it was Mr. Guthrie coming to find him. He and Tom had grown to be close friends. They enjoyed going hunting together or spending time in the barn just hanging out.

As the long days drug on and on, Emily was beginning to get bored, though. After getting her chores done, she would sit at the table and talk to Mercy while Mercy was preparing dinner, but they were running out of things to talk about, so today, she just sat at the table sipping her hot tea and gazing out the window.

"How much longer do you think winter will last?" she asked Mercy.

"Well, it's gittin' closer ta spring ever' day, Em."

"I know, but I'm bored," Emily whined. "We've been stuck in the cabin for months now. I want to go outside and do something."

"Wha's ya gonna do out dere? It's too cold ta do anyfing."

"I know, but maybe I could just take a walk around the yard or something."

"Well go 'head den, jus' let Tom knows yous out dere."

"He's in the barn with Jed," said Emily.

"I wonner wha' deys up ta all da time. Dey sho do spend a lot of time out dere."

"I think they go out there to get away from us for awhile," Emily chuckled.

"Yous prolly right," Mercy said.

Emily slipped on a pair of Tom's pants and shoved her feet into her boots. Grabbing her coat, she opened the front door. A cold blast of air hit her in the face. She shivered, but didn't let the frigid temperatures deter her from going outside. Stepping out into the yard, she stood looking at the distant mountaintops. Everywhere she looked was white. The snow was so clean and crisp looking that is almost blinded her as she took in the views.

She took a deep breath and immediately regretted it. The cold air stung her throat and lungs. She swallowed a couple of times, then turned toward the barn.

She heard Tom and Jed laughing. She was so glad they had hit it off as friends. She really liked

Jed. He was very sweet and he seemed to have taken quite a liking to Mercy. Emily saw the way he and Mercy looked at each other. She was happy for them.

She clomped her way to the barn in snow that was up to her knees. Tom had cleared a path from the house to the barn, but she opted not to walk on it. She enjoyed plowing through the snow. She grabbed up a handful of the fluffy powdery mixture and took a bite of it. It melted in her mouth.

She reached the barn and pushed the door open. Tom was sitting on a barrel whittling a small piece of wood, while Jed was leaning up against a stall door chewing on a piece of hay.

"What are you doing in here?" she asked as she approached them.

"Just hanging out and talking," Tom said. "What are you doing out here?"

"I'm bored," she said. "I needed to get out of the house for a little bit. I decided to come out and just walk around a bit."

"Well, don't wander off," Tom warned. "Stay in the yard, ok?"

"I will," she said. "I just came out to let you know I was going to be outside. Mercy made me promise to tell you."

"I'm glad you did. It's important we alway know where the other ones are in case something happens."

"I know you still get scared about us being outside alone cause of that mountain lion, but we haven't seen any animals around the place in months."

"True, but you never know when one might come around," Tom said. "Just be careful and if you see or hear anything, get to the cabin as quick as you can."

"I will," Emily said. "I promise."

She left the barn and headed up the hill toward the graveyard. It had been a long while since she stopped up to pay Frank and Nellie her respects.

As she neared the grave sites, an odd prickly feeling climbed up the back of her neck. She stopped and looked around her. Nothing was there. Everything was still and quiet. Almost peaceful. She trudged the rest of the way to the graves and stood looking down at Nellie's.

"Hi Nellie," she said. "Just wanted to let you know we are taking real good care of your farm. I think you'd be happy with how we're doing things. Each of us has our own chores and we rarely ever fight. We have stuck to your rules, too. "

A branch snapped somewhere off in the distance. Emily's head snapped around, but there was nothing there. Snow hung heavy on the tree branches and she watched as a branch broke lose from the tree and fell to the ground. That must have been what the noise was.

Turning back to the graves, she continued to talk to Nellie. She told her about the mountain lion attack and about Jed. She was just turning to leave, when she heard what sounded like snow crunching as if someone was walking on it.

She spun around again, but didn't see anything. She had the very uneasy feeling that she was being watched. She slowly scanned the area, but still did not see a single thing. Figuring it must be Tom keeping an eye on her, she just shook off the feeling and made her way back down the hill.

Mercy called from the front door that dinner was ready, so Emily quickly made her way around to the front of the house. Just as she rounded the corner, she saw Tom and Jed step out of the barn.

So it wasn't Tom up on the hill keeping an eye on her? A cold chill raced up her spine. She felt something, or someone, watching her up there. If it wasn't Tom, then who or what was it? She decided not to tell the other's about it. She didn't want them getting worried or worse yet, forbidding her to go outside alone again. Being shut up in the cabin for days on end was making her feel suffocated. If she couldn't get outside occasionally, she'd go crazy.

The evening wore on and Emily kept wondering what had been watching her up on the hill. They hadn't seen any animals around lately and Jack hadn't been through in months. What could it have been? A deer? Another mountain lion? A bear? She didn't want to worry about it, but ever since the mountain lion attacked her, she was a bit leery of another one sneaking up on her. She didn't want to be afraid though. She lived here for now and didn't want to fear being outside on her own. She quickly brushed the thought aside and joined in with the conversation as the four of them sat around the fire.

As she and Mercy curled up in bed that night, she couldn't keep her concern to herself anymore. She always told Mercy everything and this should be no exception.

"I think something was watching me out in the woods today when I went up to visit Nellie," she told her.

"Did ya sees anyfing?"

"No, nothing. It was just a feeling, really."

"Mebbe it was jus cause yous out dere alone. Mebbe yous jus sceered cause of dat mountain lion afore."

"Maybe," Emily said. "But it really creeped me out."

"Mebbe we should tell Tom," Mercy said, sitting up. "Iffn sumfing is out dere, he needs ta know."

"Let's just wait till morning," Emily said. "I don't want to bother him with it now."

"Ok, but make sho ya tells 'im in da mornin'. Don fogit."

"I won't," Emily said. "Mercy...?"

"Yeah?"

"Do you think Mr. Guthrie could be out there?"

"Nah, it's too cold," Mercy said. "He'd freeze da deaf iffn he was."

"Yeah, I suppose you're right. Good night, Mercy."

"G'night, Em," Mercy said.

Sometime during the night, Emily woke up with a full bladder. Turning over, she gently shook Mercy's shoulder.

"Mmmm," Mercy said.

"Mercy, I have to use the outhouse," Emily whispered close to her ear.

"Use da chamber pot," Mercy mumbled.

"You know I hate using that. Come outside with me to the outhouse."

"It's cold out dere. Jus use da pot."

Emily glared at Mercy in the dark. She harrumphed and rolled out of bed.

"Fine," she whispered. "I'll go by myself."

She quickly slipped on some clothes and climbed down the ladder. She was irked at Mercy. She knew that Emily hated using the pot. It made the room stink and she hated having to take it out in the morning and dump it. The outhouse was situated just behind the cabin, so she could rush out and get back before anyone even knew she was gone.

Grabbing her coat from the hook beside the door, she quietly slipped outside, pulling the door closed behind her.

The air was bitter cold. It stung Emily's face and hands, but she knew she wouldn't be out there long. It was pitch dark except for the light from the moon reflecting off the snow.

She quickly made her away around the cabin to the outhouse. Swinging the door open, she stepped in and pulled it closed behind her.

She was just finishing up her business when she heard snow crunching. She froze, listening intently for any further noise. Nothing. Maybe it was Mercy coming out to keep her company after all. She sure hoped so.

"Mercy," she called quietly through the closed door. "Is that you?"

No sound was heard. No answer from Mercy.

Emily pulled her coat tightly around her and listened some more. Another crunch. Then another. A deer, maybe? No, too loud. A bear? No, they should be hibernating.

The crunching became louder and quicker. It was coming toward the outhouse. Emily knew without a doubt that it wasn't a something, but a someone, who now stood outside the outhouse door.

She was just about to let out a scream when the door flew open and a dark form blocked the door. Before she could make a move, a large arm grabbed her around her waist at the same time a hand clamped over her mouth. She was whisked out of the outhouse and someone whispered coarsely in her ear. "Gotcha."

She was carried quickly up the hill past the graveyard and off into the woods. She was being held so tight against her captor that she couldn't kick or scream. Tears rolled down her cheeks and her stomach was in knots. She almost retched, but was suddenly dropped to the ground.

It was dark in the woods and she looked up to see who her captor was and felt a sickening feeling in the pit of her stomach. It was one of the men who worked for Mr. Guthrie. In fact, it was the man she had whacked on the head with the oar in the river.

"You!" she exclaimed, when she was able to catch her breath.

"You remember me, huh?" the man asked. "Good."

"How did you find us? What do you want?"

"Mr. Guthrie sent me. When he was released from that jail, he hung around town, secretly of course, and listened to some of the townsfolk. He heard about three kids being taken in by an old widow woman up in the mountains. It wasn't hard to figure out it was you and your little friend. We searched for a long time till we found this sweet, charming, little cabin tucked way up here at the top. We just laid low and watched for a few days. Sure enough, it was you and your blackie friend. I just needed an opportunity to nab you. I almost got you this afternoon, but missed my chance. I was just lucky to be scrolling by tonight hoping one of you would come out to tinkle and sure enough, here you come."

"Where's Mr. Guthrie?" Emily asked.

"He's gathering up more of you little brats. Seems we lost another one somewhere around here and lo, and behold, guess who I spot while scoping out the place? Seems you all made it really easy for us since you all gathered together in one spot."

"Why can't you just leave us alone?"

"Oh, I'm not after the other three. At least not yet. I'm only after you at the moment. I'll worry about the other three later."

"Why are you only after me?"

"You're the one Mr. Guthrie wants the most. You'll be a real big moneymaker for him, with you being so pretty and all."

Emily felt sick. Her head was spinning and she feared she was going to throw up. She should have just used the pot. Now look what happened. Tom was going to be so mad at her for going out without Mercy. She would probably never see her friends again.

The man grabbed her up and hauled her roughly over his shoulder. She didn't have to ask where they were going. She knew she was going to be taken back down to South Carolina to meet her fate.

They traipsed through the woods, through the deep snow to the cave where Jed had been hiding out. Emily knew it was right off of the trail that she, Mercy and Tom hiked on during better weather. But did he know that? She guessed not. He dropped her to the ground in the back of the cave and stoked a fire that he must have built before hiding out behind the cabin to wait for her to come out.

The cave was small, but it was set back enough not to be seen by any stray passersby. But who would be passing by this time of year? No one.

The flames from the fire reflected off the back wall of the cave creating dancing shadows along the wall and ceiling. It was almost mesmerizing to watch.

The heat the fire put off also radiated off the walls and created a warm, cozy temperature at the back wall.

Emily leaned against the rock and drew her knees up to her chest. What was she going to do now? The man had positioned himself between her and the opening of the cave, so she was not able to make a run for it.

The firelight cast his face in eerie shadows, but she knew he was glaring at her. He was still angry at her for hitting him with the paddle.

"We're going to stay here for the night, so make yourself comfortable."

"Where's the other man?" Emily asked.

"He got sick and headed back to our camp. No good for nothing, he is. He couldn't handle sitting out in the cold waiting for one of you to come along."

Emily's mind was running in circles. She had to find a way out of this. Maybe she'd wait till he fell asleep, then tiptoe around him and make a run for it.

He seemed to read her mind, though and said, "Don't even think about making a run for it. I'm not going to be going to sleep. It's near dawn already and I aim to head out at first light."

"Why are you so evil," Emily mumbled under her breath, but he heard her.

"Why am I so evil, you ask? I'm not evil. I'm broke. I need the money this job offers."

"Seems to me there are better ways to earn money," Emily said.

"Not so. The war has made it very difficult to find any suitable job."

"Why aren't you fighting then? Why aren't you in the Calvary?"

"I didn't want this war, so why should I fight in it?"

"Well, it's far more honorable than what you're doing."

"Shut up. Just shut up," he shouted at her. "I'm just doing what I have to do to survive."

Emily just shook her head and glared at him. "If selling children is how you want to make money, then I feel sorry for you."

"I told you to shut up!" he bellowed at her. His voice echoed around the cave and bounced off the walls.

Emily drew her legs up even tighter and wrapped her arms around them. She put her face down on her arms and cried.

Her sobbing reverberated off the walls and sounded more like a long, deep groan in the cave.

The man ignored her and poked at the fire with a stick.

Dawn was approaching. A gray, foggy light began to spread up the walls of the cave near the entrance. Emily didn't know how long they had been there, but it was probably only a couple of hours.

She glanced over at the man. He was sitting at the cave's entrance with his back to her. His back was rigid and he seemed to be listening to something.

"What is it?" she asked him.

"Sshhh," he spat out.

Emily listened but didn't hear anything.

The man suddenly jumped to his feet and peered out into the woods again. "Come on," he said to her. "We're leaving."

She didn't move toward him, so he ran over to her and grabbed her arm in a vise-like grip and jerked her toward the cave's entrance.

Stepping out of the cave, the blast of cold air took her breath away. The fire had kept the cave warm and the sudden drop in temperature was a shock to her system.

The man began dragging her through the woods. She wanted to tell him there was a path just down from the cave, but decided not to. Instead, she let him drag her over fallen logs, through heavy snow drifts and around large rocks.

Suddenly, she heard footfalls trotting up the path behind them. She tried to turn around to see who it was, but the man jerked on her arm and forced her on.

"Hey there," someone yelled.

The man ignored the call and kept on plowing through the trees, picking up speed to get away from whoever was back there.

"I said, hey there," called the voice again. "Emily recognized the voice this time."

"Jack!" she yelled. The man backhanded her. She saw stars and her head spun, but she didn't lose her footing.

The man began to drag her even faster.

A shotgun blast ripped through the air. The man stopped short and squeezed Emily's arm tight.

"I said, hey there, partner," Jack called to the man as he approached. "Now, the kindly thing to do would have been to stop and say *howdy.*"

Jack reached where they were standing and pointed his gun at the man's chest. "What's your name there, mister?" he asked, sparing a glance at Emily.

"I don't think that's any of your concern, sir," the man replied. "I'm just heading home with...my daughter, here." He yanked Emily around in front of him. He was using her as a shield against the gun.

"Is that right?" Jack asked, rubbing his beard with his hand. "Seems to me, you're dragging a girl through the woods who doesn't seem particularly interested in going with you."

"Mind your own business," growled the man. "If you don't mind, we'll be on our way now."

"Well, as a matter of fact, I do mind," said Jack. He raised his gun and leveled it at the man's chest. "Emily, come on over here with me now."

Emily started to take a step forward, but the man pulled her back.

"She ain't going nowhere, but with me," said the man.

"Is that right?" Jack said, narrowing his eyes. He took a step closer to the man and raised the gun to the man's face. "We'll see about that."

The man recoiled as he looked down the barrel of the gun, but he did not release Emily.

With lightning fast speed, the man reached behind him and pulled a pistol out of his waistband and aimed it at Jack.

In a split second, Jack fired his shotgun, hitting the man square in the face. He fell backward taking Emily with him. She screamed and everything went dark.

CHAPTER 23

Emily's eye fluttered opened. For a moment she didn't know where she was. She slowly turned her head and saw Tom, Mercy, Jed and Jack standing over her with worried expressions on their faces.

"Wha...what happened?" she asked.

"You're home now, Emily," Jack told her. "You had a horrible experience, but you're going to be ok now."

Everything suddenly came flooding back. The man, the cave, the woods...the gun fire.

Emily sprang up from the divan and took several great gulps of air. Her head was spinning and she leaned over to the side and threw up on the floor.

"She's had a real shock," Jack said. "Let's just give her a minute."

Mercy sat down on the divan next to her and put her arm around her shoulders. "It's gonna be ok, Em. Yous safe now."

Emily looked up at Tom. Was he mad at her? Did he blame her for what happened? Tom's brow was creased and his mouth was drawn up tight. She couldn't tell if he was scared or mad.

Looking at Jack, she asked, "Is he dead?"

"Yes, Emily, he is. I didn't have a choice. He was going to shoot me if I didn't shoot him first."

"I know," Emily said. "Thank you for saving me."

"These three filled me in on who that man was and what he was doing. You're lucky I came along when I did."

"What were you doing out there?" Emily asked.

"It's been several months since I checked in on you kids. I got up before dawn and was headed this way when I thought I smelled smoke. I followed the scent and I saw that man sitting at the cave entrance. I know he didn't belong, so I stepped back off the trail and just watched for a bit. When I saw him drag you out and into the woods, I followed."

"You came along at the right time," Tom said. "We cannot thank you enough."

"I'm just glad I came along when I did," Jack said. "If I hadn't have, it's hard to tell what would have happened to Emily. God be praised that I couldn't sleep last night and got on the road so early or I might have missed them."

Emily leaned on Mercy and began to cry. No one tried to stop her. They just let her cry till it passed.

"Wha'd ya do wif da man's body?" Jed asked.

"I left it there," Jack said. "I didn't have time to do anything else with it. I had to get Emily back here."

"Le's go git it buried afore da animals git it," Jed said. "He may be a bad person, but he deserves a decent restin' place."

Jack and Jed headed off to go bury the man, while Tom and Mercy stayed behind to comfort Emily.

"Are you made at me, Tom?" Emily asked once it was just the three of them.

"What? No," Tom said. "Why would I be mad?"

"Because I went outside alone," Emily said.

"Emily, I'm not mad at you. I'm just so glad you weren't hurt or taken away from us."

Tom sat down on Emily's other side and pulled her into a tight hug. "I love you Emily," he said. "I don't know what I would have done if anything would have happened to you."

The three of them sat on the divan together for a long while. Emily realized just how much she loved him and Mercy, too. She knew it would be really hard to leave them when her father came to get her, but she had them for now and she was thankful for that. She hugged them both.

After a couple of hours had passed, the three of them were beginning to worry. Jack and Jed should have been back by now. Just when Tom decided he needed to go out and look for them, they came through the door. Jed was wide eyed and nervous acting.

Mercy immediately noticed and ran over to him. "Wha's wrong, Jed?" she asked. "You look sceered."

"We ran into the man's partner while we were burying him. He didn't like the fact that we shot his friend and he pulled his gun on Jed. He was about to shoot, but I got him first," Jack said.

"You killed him too?" Emily gasped.

"Din't have no choice," Jed said. "It was him or me."

Emily sank back down on the couch. "They're both gone now," she whispered.

"Sometimes, there's no other choice," Jack said. "It's a hard fact about life. When you live out here, sometimes it's kill or be killed."

Emily nodded her understanding, but couldn't find the words to say any more.

Jack stayed with the kids for several days in case any more of Mr. Guthrie's men showed up.

After a week, he figured it was safe to head home. He told them that once the snow thawed and they were able to travel down to the town, that he would join them and they would go to the sheriff and tell him what had happened.

Life at the cabin changed. Everyone was on edge. Tom was short with everyone. Jed kept looking over his shoulder every time he stepped outside. Mercy was constantly running to a window to look outside in case someone was lurking out there and Emily refused to leave the house at all.

Weeks went by until finally one morning, the snow began to melt. The temperatures were rising and melted snow dripped down in puddles around the cabin.

Tom and Jed were out brushing the horses and noticed that they were beginning to shed their winter coats.

"It won't be long till we head to town," Tom told Jed.

"Nope. It sho won't. I be glad ta go too," said Jed. "We's bin stuck inside fo too long now."

Tom nodded his agreement and finished brushing the horse.

Emily paced the house as Mercy prepared their midday meal.

"Em, stop it," Mercy scolded her for the hundredth time. "Yous gonna wear a hole in da flo."

"I'm antsy, Mercy."

"I knowed it, but walkin' back an' forth ain't gonna help."

"I can't wait to get to town," Emily said, wringing her hands. "What if I have a telegram waiting for me from my father?"

"You'll be knowin' soon enuf."

"How long do you think it will take the snow to melt?"

"As long as it takes."

"Ugh," Emily said. "I wish it would hurry up."

It was a couple more weeks before the snow melted enough to allow travel safe. Jack showed up early one morning and that was a sure sign that it was time to go.

Emily was jittery and kept chattering at Mercy all day. Her stomach was in knots and her palms were sweaty. What would her father say in the message? Was he on his way? Was he already in town waiting for her to come down? Eager anticipation filled her. They were planning on leaving in the morning, and Emily couldn't wait.

At dawn, the wagon was hitched up and ready to go. Mercy, once again, had packed a lunch for them. Tom and Jed took the seat, while Emily and Mercy rode in the back. Jack followed along behind on his horse.

The melted snow had made everything muddy. The wagon wheels kept getting stuck and the horses hooves were throwing muck up onto the boys with every step they took.

Spring was in the air, though. The scent of pine was heavy and everywhere she looked, Emily saw signs of new life. Buds were coming out on all the trees, fawns roamed in the fields with their mothers, and the air was crisp and clean smelling.

Springtime on the mountain was breathtaking. Emily sat in the back of the wagon and took in all her surroundings. She sure would miss this place. It had become a home to her. A sadness filled her. She would miss Tom, Mercy and Jed so much. How would her life back in Pennsylvania be without them? Maybe she could come back down and visit sometime.

They finally reached the town by late morning. Tom steered the team toward the sheriff's office and hitched them to a post while he and Jed ran in to see if the sheriff was there.

Jack, Emily and Mercy joined them inside and they explained to the sheriff what had happened.

"So they're both dead?" he asked Jack.

"Yes sir. Both of them."

"Well, nothing we can do about it now. You say it was in self defense?"

"Yes sir, it was. Emily and Jed can both testify to that."

"Well, you'll be glad to know that your old friend, Mr. Guthrie, was picked up a couple of towns over for trying to kidnap the sheriff's daughter. He won't be getting released this time. Judge said he'll be thrown in jail and will be spending a long time there. So, it looks like you kids shouldn't have anymore trouble out of him."

Emily let out a sigh of relief. Mercy sagged into her and Emily saw a tear run down her face. "You ok?" she asked her.

"Yeah. I's jus' so glad we wone haf ta worry no mo 'bout all dat."

"Me too, Mercy," Emily said. "Me too."

The sheriff asked Jack to stick around for a day or two so when the judge came back through town, he could explain everything to him. Jack agreed and they all left the sheriff's office.

As they stepped out onto the street, the sheriff called from the doorway. "Oh, Emily," he said. "You might want to go see the Postmaster. I believe he has something for you."

Emily dashed off for the Post Office as fast as her feet would carry her. Tom, Mercy and Jed followed, but weren't able to keep up.

She burst through the Post Office's door. Gasping and trying to catch her breath, she approached the window. Tom, Mercy and Jed walked through the door about that time.

"Sir," Emily said between gasps. "Do you have a message for me?"

The postman looked at her and his face suddenly registered who she was. Her heart sank when the look on his face turned from one of recognition to one of deep sadness. "Yes...yes I do. Let me find it here." He dug around on his desk and finally produced a small slip of paper. Handing it to her, he averted his eyes.

Emily grabbed the paper from his hand and read it out loud. *"Dear Miss Emily Dunn, We regret to inform you that your father has passed away. He was killed in an accident at the mill. A representative for his Last Will and Testament will be arriving soon to handle the case. Our sincere apologies, The Dunn Iron Works committee."*

The paper slipped from Emily's fingers and floated to the floor.

Stunned silence filled the room. No one knew what to say to her or what to do to help her.

Silent tears streamed down her face. Her father was gone. Gone. Forever. She was all alone.

The Postmaster cleared his throat behind her and she slowly turned to look at him.

"Miss, the attorney arrived a few days ago. He's been staying at the hotel over the restaurant waiting for you to arrive in town."

Emily simply nodded and walked outside into the street. Tom, Mercy and Jed followed her.

"Em?" Mercy asked.

"Yeah..." Emily said.

"We's here fo ya iffn ya needs us. Yous not alone. Yous got Tom, Jed and me."

Emily nodded absently and headed across the street to the restaurant.

Everything seemed a blur. Bessie had ran upstairs to get the attorney while the kids took seats at a table.

Emily couldn't wrap her mind around the fact that her father was dead. He died never knowing what happened to her. She would never see him again. Tears welled up in her eyes and spilled, unchecked, down her cheeks.

The attorney found his way to the table where they all sat. He noticed all four of them and cleared his throat. "I'm sorry kids, but you'll have to leave Emily and me while I discuss the will. I hope you understand."

Tom nodded and ushered the other two toward the door. "Em, we'll be outside when you're done."

Again, Emily only nodded, looking down at her hands.

The attorney took a seat and riffled through his satchel until he found the papers he was looking for. Laying them out on the table, he cleared his throat again.

"Emily, I'm Mr. Brooks, I was your father's attorney. I will read the Last Will and Testament of your father in it's entirety, then I will explain it all to you. Do you understand?"

It irked her that he was talking to her like she was stupid, but she merely looked up at him and nodded.

It took several minutes for him to read the will. When he finally laid it down, he folded his hands in front of him and looked her directly in the eye. "Do you understand what I just read to you. Do you know what it means?"

Emily had no idea what all the fancy words and statements meant, so she shook her head at him.

"It means, my dear, that you inherit everything. You were his sole beneficiary."

"What do I inherit? The house?"

"You inherit *everything* that belonged to your father. The house, the iron works mill, the money...*everything.*"

"What am I going to do with all that?"

"Well, as your father's attorney, and now yours, I would advise you to sell the house and the iron works. You are too young to run a business and that house is way too big for you to live in all alone."

"What about Olive? She could live there with me."

"Olive has found other gainful employment, my dear. She is no longer at the house."

"When did my father die?" Emily asked, blandly.

"Late last summer. Just a few weeks after you disappeared. We've been searching for you for months. If it hadn't been for your telegram, I'm not sure we would have found you. I was informed by your friend, Bessie, what all has happened to you. I am so sorry. I know you have been through a lot."

"What do I do now, sir?" Emily choked back a sob.

"If you want me to, I can handle the sale of the house and mill. You won't have to do a thing. When the sales are complete, I will wire the money to any bank you want me to."

Emily just stared at him in shock. "I...I guess...if that's what you think I should do."

"I do."

Emily thought for a moment. Where would she go? What would she do? She glanced out the window and saw her friends standing out by the street. They were talking back and forth and occasionally one of them would laugh.

"Yes...yes sir," she said almost absentmindedly. "Please sell the house and mill. Transfer the money to the bank here, please."

"Here?" he asked her, surprised. "You're going to stay here? Maybe you don't understand. You're rich. Very wealthy, actually. You could go anywhere you wanted. Are you sure you want to stay here?"

"I'm right where I'm supposed to be, sir. This is my home."

He stared blankly at her for a moment, then shoved some papers in her direction. "Then all I need you to do is sign these papers and I will take care of the rest."

Emily scratched her name on the paper and pushed them back in his direction. "Thank you for your help, Mr. Brooks. I truly appreciate it."

"I'll send a telegram letting you know when the funds are deposited," Mr. Brooks said. "Again, Miss Emily, I am so sorry for your loss."

Emily left the restaurant and headed outside to join her friends.

The ride back up the mountain passed by in a blur. Emily was heartbroken and confused. She didn't tell the others what the attorney had told her. She didn't care about the money. She didn't really want it.

They arrived back at the cabin right before nightfall.

While Tom and Jed put the horses up, Emily climbed the ladder to the loft and found the old bag that Mary had given them. It felt like so long ago when this journey began.

She dug around in the bag until her hand found what she was looking for. Pulling out the compass, she stuffed it into the pocket of her dress and went back outside. On the way, she grabbed Mercy by the hand and quietly led her to the spot in the front yard where the view stretched on forever. It was Emily's favorite place on the farm.

Standing at the edge of the mountain, Emily looked out at a sky streaked with hues of pink, yellow and orange. The sun was almost set, making the mountains off in the distance appear to be on fire. She knew now. She knew she was home. She knew this is where she belonged.

Opening the compass, she held it out in front of her. The arrow was pointing directly toward the distant mountains in front of her.

"Mercy," she said. "We began this journey heading North. I always figured North meant Pennsylvania. It didn't. It meant up...up into the mountains. This is the end of our journey north. We're home now."

About the Author

Carol Hall is an American writer who grew up in Chester, West Virginia, but now lives in the mountains of Tennessee.

Carol was inspired to write by her father who loved to tell tall tales to her and her two sisters, as well as to his grandchildren.

Carol's hobbies are reading, hiking, exploring new places and spending time with her family and friends and her three cats.

For more information or to contact Carol, please write to her at,

khiris@att.net